I0664241

HOLLY'S RELUCTANT COWBOY

Cowboys of Wildcat Creek, Book Four

BARBARA MCMAHON

Holly's Reluctant Cowboy
Copyright © 2022 Barbara McMahon
All Rights Reserved

1

Cody Fallon pulled the wire taut, straining against the lever to take up any slack. Jose nailed in the staple holding the barbed wire against the fence post. Once set, he nodded, and Cody released the wire stretcher. Taking off his hat, he swiped his arm against his forehead.

"I'm so hot I'm about to melt," he said.

"Si. Once we're finished, I'm heading for the river."

Jose put his hammer on his belt and wiped his own sweating forehead.

"Good idea. The way I feel, I could jump in boots and all."

Cody reset his hat and picked up the wire stretcher.

"That's the last of this section. Two more and we can call it a day."

He walked along the repaired section of fencing originally put up by his great-grandfather close to ninety years ago. Except for patching here and there, the fence had been bull tough and seen ninety years of rain, snow, baking heat and range cattle. He knew it had taken his great-grandpa Fallon years to fence in the acres the family claimed of wild Wyoming land. Before he settled there, cattle had run free, but changing times called for deeded land to be fenced and kept intact.

As he walked along the rough ground, unwilling to go

back to the truck until he was done, he wondered what the man would think of the spread today. His grandpa had bought out two neighboring ranches. His mom had brought acreage to the marriage.

He almost smiled. He could hear her telling his dad to watch out, or she'd leave and take her land with her any time they had a fight.

As if.

He remembered being so embarrassed as a teenager with the lovey-dovey actions of his parents—no matter where or when. Now he had total respect for the love they shared, wondering if he'd ever fall as hard for a woman as his dad had for his mom.

"Last section," Jose said as he tested the sagging barbed wire between two poles a short time later.

"None too soon for me. I'd much rather ride tally on the herd than do this," Cody said, threading the wire into the wire stretcher. He could almost feel the coolness of the river. It wasn't any hotter than any other August. This year the water still ran cool.

A working ranch had more chores than he could list. Some he liked, some he tolerated and some he flat out wouldn't do. Riding fence fell into the tolerated list. He and Jose worked together tightening the strands until the section was solid again. The cut beneath his eye smarted again as perspiration poured down his cheeks. The only thing worse than blazing hot summer was freezing cold Wyoming winters.

Once finish with the last section, he shouldered the wire stretcher. They began heading back to the truck parked near the first section they'd fixed earlier that afternoon. It was more than a mile away, but Cody'd rather walk it than hop in the truck after every section, moving it a few dozen feet and then getting out to repair that section and then getting back in again.

A puff of air gave an illusion of coolness, immediately forgotten beneath the hot sun. The two of them were almost back to the truck when Cody saw one of the ranch hands riding toward them. He dumped the stretcher in the back of the truck, shucked his gloves and tossed them in, too.

Jose took two bottles of cold water from the cooler, tossed one to Cody and drank from his.

Cody started to lean against the side of his truck. A split second against the hot metal ended that. He took a long drink as he watched Aaron ride closer. He hoped Jared hadn't come up with some other task that had to be done. That river was calling his name.

The older man pulled up near Cody and nodded.

"You boys done here?"

Cody nodded, taking a last sip of the bottle, tossing the empty in the back of the truck. "What's up?"

"The new hand said he saw some cattle he didn't think were ours. And a couple of horses. You seen anything like that?"

"No, where'd he see them?"

"He can't remember. Don't know why your dad hired him. He couldn't find his bed at night if he wasn't already in the bunkhouse."

Aaron shook his head in disgust and looked in the distance.

"Anyway, I'm trying to find out where that might be and

whose cattle. Don't know why there'd be any horses loose on the range. Not one of ours, that's for sure. But I guess I have to give him the benefit of the doubt that he knows the difference between a horse and steer."

Cody shrugged and turned to look at the horizon in all directions. He also wondered why his father had hired Billy Bob Dalton before he'd left for a world cruise he'd been promising his wife for years.

Sometimes Cody thought it was to drive him and his brothers crazy while they were gone. But family solidarity was strong and he wasn't going to side against his father with anyone–even a long time ranch hand like Aaron.

"Where was he working when he saw these animals?" Cody asked.

Maybe he'd drive around to see if he spotted anything.

"He left to go with Pedro to check that watering hole near Martin's place. Then Pedro sent him on some dumb fool errand and he got lost. I think he just gave his horse his head and that got him back to the barn. So I haven't a clue where he was. And Pedro isn't back yet or I'd have his head."

Cody nodded, hiding a smile. He knew the old timers would haze the new guy. And Billy Bob was so gullible he was an easy mark. Not that it made it easier to get things done, but they'd tire of it soon enough and settle into a routine.

"Jose and I will head over toward the north pasture, see if we spot anything. If not, it'll have to keep. We've got a date with the river."

"Know what you're saying. It's so blasted hot today."

Cody waited for Jose to get in the cab and then headed toward the next pasture over. The windows were rolled down, the air circulating as hot as steam. Nothing would cool them off except sun going down. Or the river.

Cody beat a tattoo on the steering wheel, trying to find the coolest spots to hold. The truck lurched and bounced and shimmied. Twice he hit his head on the roof. Jose never said a word, braced as best he could next to him. He tried to think of who could have cattle running in their spread.

The neighboring ranches all took as much care about property fences as the Rocking F did. Cody ran into them from time to time, lending a hand the same as they would if he were repairing a section and they happened by. The whole point of the fences were to keep the cattle separated.

And he didn't know anyone who let horses run free. Sure, loose in a corral, or even in a paddock close to the barn like Mickelson did. But not free running on open range.

Was Billy Bob seeing things? Maybe he didn't know the difference between a horse and a steer.

The truck lurched its way up the small hill. From the top he could see in all directions. Toward the east the slow moving pumpers bobbed their heads up and down drawing oil from the ground. He'd have to check those fences in another few days. Make sure none of them were weak. One of their steers had gotten injured a few years back in some of the mechanisms of an oil pumper.

Looking toward the north he spotted a good portion of the herd, spread out as they grazed. The pumper didn't bother them. There were a few trees dotting the land but only a few head were taking advantage of the shade. Nothing looked like a horse. And from this distance, he couldn't differentiate any cattle that looked any different from what he expected to see.

Gazing toward the west he saw trees and open land. It was south where the line of trees followed the river. He could almost feel the shade from here, the coolness of the water.

"The heck with this," he murmured, turning the truck. "We're heading for the river, Jose."

"About time," the man grumbled.

It was after five by the time they reached that bend in the river where Cody's grandfather had fashioned a swimming hole of sorts. He'd carted in rocks, dug it out a bit, and made it as deep as possible even in the long hot days of summer.

"Figures," Cody grumbled as he drew to a stop near the bank. There were already three horses standing in the shade, cowboy hats and boots nearby and the owners splashing and yelling in the water.

"I swear Kyle wouldn't know a full day's work if it bit him on the butt," he said climbing out of the truck, already shrugging out of his shirt. Boots and jeans followed in less than one minute. Then he took off running to the ledge that gave the best diving position. Letting out a wild cowboy yell, he cannon balled into the water, dousing everyone.

"Kept the water cool for you," his brother Kyle called out when he surfaced.

"While I was keeping the ranch going for you," Cody retaliated, skimming his hand on the surface sending a sheet of water in Kyle's face.

The battle was on and sides were drawn, the water fight going until Cody thought he was half drowned. Not that he was going to stop but darn it when had he gotten so old he even considered stopping before the rest?

Finally it wound down.

"That your hat?" Jose said standing in water up to his neck and nodding to the hat drifting around the bend.

Cody swore and took off after the hat, to the laughter of the men behind him. He should have taken it off before hitting the water. He was around the bend of the slow moving river before he caught up with it. Slamming it on his head, he tread water for a moment, then struck out for shore. The cool water felt good. Here the voices of the others were muted. He sat in the shade, feet still dangling in the water, watching it go by and trying to summon enough gumption to get up to head for the house.

Lying back on the dried grass, shifting a bit to get half way comfortable on the rough ground, Cody looked up through the leaves to the clear blue sky. Nothing better than ranching, he thought.

How men could be happy going to a nine-to-five job, stuck in some high rise office day in and day out was beyond him. He bet none of them had a river they could swim in whenever they wanted.

"Hey, we thought you drowned," Kyle said, floating on the river.

"So you came to save me?" Cody asked, raising up on one elbow.

"Heck, no. I was the only one not afraid to discover the body."

He swam over to where he could stand and walked out of the river to flop down beside Cody.

"Jose told me about Aaron looking for some cattle not ours. And Billy Bob's stellar report."

Cody lay back down. "Yeah, he probably imagined it. Or

it was on Morgan's land and he couldn't see the fence. Tell me you fathom why dad hired him."

"Can't see it myself. But what's more confusing is why Jarred won't fire him."

"Hmmm." Cody wondered the same thing. "Give him time, something's bound to finally break."

"Maybe. I'm done and heading back."

"Hmmm."

"You going to sleep?" Kyle asked, plunging back into the river.

"Naw, I'll be along in a minute."

Code sat up, contemplating walking back to the truck versus swimming. No contest. The water felt good even working against the current to get back to the swimming hole. The others were in various stages of dress when he stepped out. He took his shirt to rough dry, then tossed it into the back of the truck. He'd just wear his jeans home, couldn't get any hotter now that he'd left the water.

When he got back, he wanted to talk to Billy Bob. Maybe the kid would have remembered some detail that would pinpoint where he'd been that day.

Cody entered the bunkhouse right at six thirty. No one was late to chuck. Carlos had been cooking for the Rocking F Ranch for the last fifteen years. With Cody's parents gone for most of the coming year, he and his brothers now ate with the men.

Saved them making their own meals.

Cooking was one of the never do things on Cody's list. He'd eat cold cereal morning, noon and night rather than cook.

The men were sitting at the long table and he took a place near the end. Jarred was at the other end, Kyle about mid way down. The rest of the men were hired hands. Billy Bob sat across from him. Perfect. Once everyone had heaped their plates with potatoes, beans, beef and corn, he began to eat.

"Tell me about seeing those cattle earlier," Cody said.

Billy Bob looked up, his eyes widening as if afraid to say the wrong thing.

"I saw a bunch. Looked scrawny and thin. And there were three horses, too. Skinniest things I ever saw."

"Where exactly?"

Billy Bob ducked his head.

"I don't know my way around too good yet."

"You've been here four months. When are you going to learn your way around?" Cody asked more sharply than he intended.

He seemed to get annoyed faster with this young man than anyone else he knew.

"I don't know. Everything all looks the same to me," Billy Bob said, ducking his head.

He scooped up a big fork full of beans and began chewing as if to ward off any more questions.

Cody took a couple of bites of his own and then tried a different tactic.

"Describe the field."

"Huh?"

"Was it flat or rolling? Did it have trees? Was it near the river or farther from the homestead? Were there lots of other cattle or none? Near the pumpers? You must have registered something."

Billy Bob scrunched up his face as if thinking. Then he brightened.

"No pumpers. But a bunch of trees, not in a row like the ones by the river, but clumped together, you know in a mini-forest."

Mini forest? Cody almost smacked his head. There were copses of trees, individual trees, and a line of trees near the river. Still, he thought about the description.

"Maybe near Braddock's ranch?" he asked.

"Huh?"

"West, the ranch on the western boundary of our land. There's grove a trees there near where we have a well. Did you see a windmill?"

Billy Bob stared at him for a minute then smiled. "I did, behind the trees one stuck up."

Cody nodded.

Several of the others had stopped talking to listen, then his brother Jarred spoke. "Near Braddock's then. You want to ride over there and check it out?"

"Tomorrow."

"There's enough daylight left today," he said.

Cody looked at him.

"Then you go. I'm done for today."

"It won't take long."

"Then you go," Cody repeated.

Jarred's lips tightened as he glared at Cody.

Cody met the implied challenge with a look of his own.

Jarred was a year older and their father had left him with two votes in running the ranch while they were on the cruise—in case there were situations that needed a deciding vote. Cody didn't acknowledge that Jarred had any more right to run the place than he or Kyle or Tyler did. As far as Cody was concerned, the four brothers had an equal share in running the Rocking F, and notwithstanding what Jarred thought, Cody wasn't working for him.

"How's Frank doing?" Aaron asked.

"Not good," Seth Johnson said.

"You visit him recently?" Jarred asked.

"Two days ago, as I told you at dinner that night. Why you boys don't listen is beyond me."

Cody smiled as he looked at his grandfather. It was a familiar refrain. Had he mentioned visiting their neighbor in the convalescent hospital? He didn't remember. Sometimes grandpa thought he told them something when he didn't.

The tense moment eased as the topic changed.

"And the update?" Jarred asked.

"He's not doing well. He's conscious and all, but can't talk. Or what he says is gibberish." Seth shook his head. "Many a day your dad and Frank, Paul Martin and I worked roundups together. He's your dad's age, too young to have a stroke. I know he's worried about the ranch."

"So who runs his place?" Billy Bob asked.

"He has a hand, Ed Stinner," Jarred said.

Seth shook his head. "Lot of work for one man."

"Maybe he needs to check the fence," Cody said. "I'll ride out in the morning to see if the cattle Billy Bob saw belong to the Bar-B-Bar. Maybe I can find the breach and fix it myself after I drive the cattle back."

"And the horses," Billy Bob added.

"Now that's downright odd, if true," Pedro said. "No one lets horses run free, not if they need them for work."

Cody nodded. Time enough to find out the situation in the morning. Right now he wanted more dinner. Carlos could cook up mighty fine meals. And it sure beat cereal.

2

Cody saddled up his favorite gelding early the next morning and headed out for the west field. It was about a twenty minute ride, but the sun hadn't gotten up too high in the sky and the morning felt crisp and cool. He knew he and his brothers should visit Frank Braddock as well as his grandfather. His father would expect no less. Neighbors rallied around neighbors. He'd stop in the next time he was in town.

He wasn't much for hospitals. And it had to suck to be bedridden even for a short time. He hadn't seen Frank in a while. Maybe since last Christmas. He had celebrated with the Fallons.

Fact was, Cody couldn't remember the last time he'd been at the Braddock place. Frank was his father's friend. If he came to dinner or holidays, it was always understood they invited him over because he couldn't host their noisy clan on his own.

Cody tried to remember if Frank had any family. Wasn't there a kid somewhere? Frank had been divorced as long as Cody could remember, but he thought his dad said something about a kid. Or maybe it was another rancher and Cody was getting them mixed up.

When he opened and closed the gate that led to the

pasture Billy Bob had identified, Cody saw the horse right away–a bay looking off his feed. The animal ambled right toward him. When he drew closer, Cody could see how thin he was. Range feed wasn't enough or the horse had worms, or both.

"Hey, fellow, what're you doing out here?"

The horse nosed his own mount then walked a couple more steps so Cody could scratch his ears. Easing his lariat from his saddle so not to spook the horse, he shook the loop around the horse's neck and wrapped the other end around the saddle horn.

"Come on, fella, I'll take you home."

Keeping alert he soon saw the cattle. Maybe twenty head, some beneath the trees though the heat of the day had only begun. Others grazed on the dried grass. Then he saw another horse, standing by the water trough fed by the windmill. The horse whinnied and watched with ears forward as Cody rode nearer.

"So there are a couple of you after all," he whispered.

The horse had a gash on his hind quarters and was as thin as the one next to Cody.

He studied the line of fencing but from this position nothing looked out of place. No glaring gap showed.

"Come on, then, let's see if I can find a breach."

He let the first horse sip at the trough and shook his rope off him.

He rode to the fence and began riding beside it. After ten minutes he found a make shift gate that was opened. A western gate that was barbed wire attached to poles that hooked to the fence posts. Somehow this one had gotten undone and let the animals cross to Fallon land.

And probably caused the injury to the one horse to boot.

He dismounted far enough away from the tangle of barbed wire to keep his horse safe, and tried to get the gate out of the way. Finally giving up, he pulled wire cutters from his back pocket and cut the wire away. He coiled it up best he could, and tucked it near a post to keep it as far from the range animals as possible. When he came back to fix it, he'd take the old wire and dispose of it where it wouldn't harm anything.

Remounting he rounded up the two horses and led them onto Braddock land. The horses followed willingly.

If he remembered right, a south west direction should put him in line with the home place for Frank Braddock. He studied the land as he rode, going slowly for the horses. Both looked like they had little energy or stamina. The sooner they were back in their corral and fed some grain, the better they'd both be.

Twenty minutes later he saw Braddock's barn. Then the house. As he came closer he saw the corral was empty. Where were the rest of the horses? Had they all gotten out?

Behind him the injured horse followed picked up the pace. The other kept following with his slow steady gait.

Cody felt he was an easy-going guy most of the time, but not when the welfare of animals was concerned. There was no excuse for not taking care of ranch animals.

Holly Braddock finished her bottle of water. Biting off another bit of granola bar, she gazed out the kitchen window at the barn behind the house. Nothing was going as she expected. And if things didn't change soon, she'd have to give up and go back home.

She finished the granola bar and tossed the wrapper in the trash. Grabbing her purse, she dug out her keys. She'd be early to see her father, but if she left now she'd have a chance for a cup of coffee at Rosie's Café before visiting her dad. Glancing around the worn kitchen, she shook her head. How had it changed so much from when she was younger?

Or had it? Maybe she just remembered it differently. Kids didn't care about the latest appliances in the kitchen or an immaculately painted house. But it sure looked more rundown that she ever expected.

She also expected the power to be on. She'd stopped by the convalescent home yesterday when she arrived, but her father had been sleeping. Even though she stayed for a couple of hours, he didn't wake up and she didn't want to waken him.

Arriving here after a quick meal in town, it had dismayed her to discover no electricity. She remembered a generator near the pump house, but hadn't a clue how to operate it.

So no coffee this morning. No shower since the pump didn't work. Nothing to eat beyond dry stale cereal and her granola bars. The food in the refrigerator had spoiled enough to make her almost sick when she dumped it last night.

She hoped she could get the power back on today. But first she wanted to visit her father. She couldn't believe how frail he'd looked yesterday. He had IV tubes for nourishment as his ability to swallow had been impeded the nurse said. And he didn't communicate well yet, she'd been told.

Fear gripped her for a moment. He couldn't die. She loved her father. He was too young to die—especially when she hadn't seen him in months and hadn't visited the ranch in a dozen years.

Which wasn't my fault, she thought as she headed out the back door. She'd asked to come many times, but her father always said it was such a treat to meet her in Palm Springs or Los Angeles or San Francisco that she didn't argue too strongly.

She loved coming to visit as a child. Her mother loathed her visits, but it had been a magical place to Holly. She got to ride horses all day long, hang out around cowboys and pretend she belonged always, not just for summer visits.

How her mother didn't adore cowboys, Holly didn't understand. She'd had such a crush on them when she last visited. She'd been fourteen at the time and so wanted to be grown up. Now she was. And nothing was as she remembered.

As she approached the rental car, she heard horses in the distance. That had been something she wondered about, where the animals were. Since neighbors looked out for each other, she believed someone had come for her father's stock to care for it while he was incapacitated.

She tossed her bag into the car through the open window and watched as a cowboy riding a big chestnut horse followed by two others came nearer. She walked toward the corral figuring that is where he'd be heading.

"Good morning," she called when he was closer.

"Ma'am," he replied, touching the rim of his hat with two fingers.

She watched as his gaze skimmed over her, a hint of a smile tugging at his lips. What was wrong with her clothes? She had on new jeans, new boots and a western checked shirt. Just what cowboys wore.

And as far from the designer dresses her mother preferred as possible to get.

"These horses were on our land. Don't know how they got there, but one's injured."

He led them right into the corral. Leaning over, he reached for the gate, moving his horse along with the gate until he latched it shut.

Holly looked at the horses. They were in terrible shape, gaunt looking with ribs clearly showing. One had a bloody flank.

"Are you sure they belong on the Braddock ranch?" she asked, feeling totally unprepared to deal with livestock. "I thought neighbors had taken the stock to care for while my father's recovering."

He looked down at her, his hat pulled low on his forehead. The blazing blue eyes that gazed at her from his tanned face sparked a memory.

"You're a Fallon," she said. She remembered her father talking about the bright blue eyes of the Fallons.

"Right you are, Cody Fallon at your service. And you are?" he replied.

"Holly Braddock. Frank Braddock is my dad."

"Hmm."

He glanced around and Holly immediately felt defensive. She knew he was taking in the peeling paint on the clapboard, the dead plants surrounding the house. Even the barn looked as if it were sagging.

"Where's Ed?' he asked, looking back at her.

"Who's Ed?"

"Ed Stinner, the man who worked this place with your dad?"

"I have no idea. There was no one here when I arrived yesterday. And from the looks of things, no one has been around anytime recently."

His steady gaze was unnerving. She brushed back a strand of hair.

"So who's taking care of things?" he asked.

Without warning, the words burst forth.

"I am."

Good grief, what she knew about cattle ranching would cover a dime, maybe.

"I mean I guess it would be me until my dad's better," she clarified.

"Then you need to get these horses some feed and fill that water tank."

She glanced at the dusty tank in the corral. Both horses were standing nearby as if waiting for it to miraculously fill with water. She bit her lower lip. Where was the nearest hose?

"Yes, I'll do that."

"Need any help fixing that gash on the flank?"

"Shouldn't I call a vet?" she asked, eyeing the cut.

The blood had dribbled down the back leg but seemed to ooze rather than stream. She hadn't the slightest idea how to care for it.

"Clean it up and we'll see. It's already scabbing over. And he didn't limp on the walk here so my guess is he'd be good to go in no time. Just check it and sprinkle some antiseptic on it."

"Antiseptic, right." What antiseptic?

"You visit here often?" Cody asked.

"Not lately."

He studied her another minute, then dismounted. Looping the reins over the top rail of the corral, he glanced at her.

"Do you know where anything is?"

She felt as if he'd judged her and found her wanting. He'd pegged it, though. She didn't know where anything was but saddles and bridles for riding. She'd never had the need before.

"No. I just got here last night." And it was early. She hadn't even had much for breakfast.

No sense trying to fool this cowboy, he looked as if he'd see through her in a heartbeat.

He lifted his hat and ran his fingers through his dark hair, then reset the hat.

"Come on, then." he said, heading for the wide double doors of the barn.

"I was going in to town to see my dad," she said, glancing at her watch.

"Yeah, well I was going to work my place this morning. You take care of your animals first."

She heard him mutter something under his breath but couldn't make it out. Taking a breath, she followed.

He paused at the doorway and she almost bumped into him. Catching herself in time, she side stepped and then stopped. Why had he?

"Tack room is there," he said.

"Yes." She knew that much.

He stomped over and stepped inside, reappearing a moment later with a hose slung over his shoulder. "Faucet's on the outside," he said.

Holly felt like a puppy in training following him back outside. She needed to take control of the situation, but hadn't a clue how to do so.

In seconds, he had the hose connected. Thrusting the end into her hands, he pointed to the trough. She dragged the hose over and barely had it over the edge of trough before she heard the squeak of the faucet handle.

Nothing happened.

She looked over at him.

"There's no water."

Stating the obvious was not the way to make a good impression.

"Why not?"

He jiggled the handle again, turning it off and on. Nothing.

She cleared her throat.

"The power's off. The pump isn't working."

She heard an expletive then watched as Cody stomped off toward the pump house. What—he didn't believe her?

Five minutes later she heard the roar of the generator. A moment later water gushed through the hose. Both horses ambled closer, one sticking its head in the water taking a long drink.

She wanted to fling the hose into the tank and dash toward the house to fill every container she could with water.

She tried to remember if she left any faucets open.

Cody came back as she watched the water rise in the tank.

"Eww, it's dirty," she said. The water tank had a layer of dust on the bottom, now floating on the water as it rose.

"They don't care. It's the water they want. How long's the power been off?"

"I don't know. I just got here last night."

He nodded and disappeared back into the barn. Holly held the hose wondering how long it would take to fill the tank. Especially if the horses, now both of them, were drinking at the same time.

Cody came from the barn, a couple of flakes of hay on his shoulder. He tossed them over the fence and the horses left the tank to eat.

"You have little left. And I didn't see any grain."

Another thing to worry about. No food for her and none for these horses. So much for her plans to stay the night in town. She couldn't leave until she made arrangements for the care of the horses. She hoped her father had an address book or something that would clue her in to who his friends were. If she could get the phone number of someone to watch the horses, she would call them before heading for town. At least the cattle could fend for themselves on the range. Or so she believed.

Couldn't the horses?

"Hey!"

She looked at him. Had he been talking?

"What?"

"I asked about the other horses," he said.

"What other horses? I didn't even know about these two."

Cody's lips tightened.

"I'll check the bunk house. If Ed's pulled his freight, he probably turned them loose to forage for themselves. However, that's not a good idea. From the looks of their feet, they need a farrier soon. There could be others out on the range needing care, too."

He looked exasperated as he turned and headed for the bunk house, the small dormitory like building on the far side of the barn. It housed up to ten cowboys.

What had happened to all the cowboys? Shouldn't Ed still be here running things? Maybe he took a couple of days off and would return soon. But she expected more than one cowboy working. Another question to ask her dad.

Especially if this Cody Fallon expected her to ride the range looking for horses. While she'd ridden horses every day when she visited her father, it was always with him. She didn't know how vast the ranch was, in which direction horses would have gone, nor how to get them back to the corral. She couldn't imagine herself getting them to follow her back like Cody Fallon had done.

"He's gone," Cody said walking back.

Each step sent a small puff of dust from the ground. It was dry and growing hotter by the minute. Yesterday had been a scorcher, today promised more of the same. She yearned for the air conditioned convalescent hospital, not the dusty hot ranch house.

"Then it's up to me, I guess. I'll go look for the horses after I visit my Dad."

She hoped he'd be awake and alert when she visited so she could get the answers to all the questions she had.

He nodded, glancing at the water tank. He rocked back on his heels, looking at her again.

The trough was more than half full. She kept the hose steady, conscious of his gaze, of his impatience. Now what?

"You know the horses need to be fed twice a day, right? Make sure you give them clean hay, no moldy stuff. What I saw in the barn looks good. Give them a flake each. And you need to pick up some grain when you're in town. They're way too thin. Feed them some of that each day until they regain their normal weight. And call the farrier."

She smiled politely and nodded–not having a clue who the farrier was. She'd ask her father how to do things and who to call. She didn't need this cowboy talking to her like she was three.

"Thank you for bringing the horses home."

She hoped he took the hint and left. She'd find out on her own how to manage. Or even if she needed to. Her father probably had things covered and she just needed to learn what.

He ran his fingers through his hair again, replaced his hat and went to his horse. Effortlessly he mounted.

"Say hey to your father for us. We'll each be by to visit next time we're in town."

She nodded, and looked back at the water coming from the hose, her mind churning with all the questions she had. For a moment uncertainty hit. She knew nothing about running a ranch. She hadn't even known where the hose was, how could she think she could manage even for a day or two?

But she wouldn't let this cowboy know.

"I'll tell him," she replied, her gaze on the water lest she end up studying him like he'd been studying her.

Cute as all get out, in a rough and tumble way. Broad shoulders, long muscular legs encased in jeans and dusty boots. The cowboy hat made anyone look good, but was especially enticing on Cody Fallon. The startling blue eyes could have her mesmerized given half a chance.

Yet he evidenced no interest in her beyond instructions on what probably every kid within a hundred miles was born knowing–how to feed and care for a horse.

"There are maybe twenty head of cattle on our land, same breach in the fence north east of here. I'll push them back today and mend the fence. You might run a tally to make sure they're all back. Let me know."

She regretted even more the years she hadn't visited. A tally sounded like counting the cattle. How in the world did someone do that if they were moving around while they grazed. What if one got counted twice or another not at all?

"Thank you."

She hadn't a clue where the pasture was he was talking about, much less how to mend a barbed wire fence. Thank goodness he was going to do that.

Hearing the horse move away, she peeked after Cody Fallon as he left the way he came.

"Oh, Daddy, you've got to get better soon if you want to keep this place running. I'm not the girl to do it," she whispered as the water reached the top of the trough. She tossed the running hose on the ground and hurried to shut the water off.

Going to the house, she was grateful for the generator. She filled pots and pans in the kitchen. Then went through the house and flushed all the toilets and considered filling the bath tub, but stopped short of that. She'd see to getting the electricity turned back on while she was in town. In the meantime, she gave thanks Cody had known about the generator.

Heading for the car, she wondered what would have

happened if he'd found no one at the ranch? Would he have left the horses hoping someone would return, or taken them to his place?

Holly paid attention to the scenery as she drove to town. It was so different from where she lived in California. She noticed the fencing along the road; the dirt driveways leading off, back beyond the rolling hills. How many ranches were in the area? How large was her father's ranch? Hadn't he wanted her to take over for him when he was ready to retire? She was his only child.

Though her mother would have a heart attack if she could hear her daughter's thoughts. She'd tried so hard all the years since the divorce to eradicate any trace of the ranch from Holly's life. According to her mother, she'd made a monumental mistake thinking she had any idea of what being a rancher's wife entailed. It was a horrible existence and she wised up before Holly was three and left it and Frank behind.

Holly wasn't privy to the settlement they reached, but she and her mother lived well in Palms Springs which her mother adored. She played golf and tennis, belonged to the best country club and enjoyed all the social activities offered.

Holly had enjoyed a life of privilege growing up, taking everything for granted–even her contentious parents fighting via long distance. She'd loved the summer visits on the ranch, had often told her father she wanted to live with him, but neither he nor her mother had taken her seriously.

Once in high school she made great friends and her life revolved around her own social activities. Then college. The year long trip to Europe from her father upon graduation had been unexpected, but delightful. She'd relished every moment.

Now she had serious questions. Had he beggared the ranch to send her to Europe? Why else would it be in such disrepair? Or had he been ill far longer than anyone suspected?

And why were there no cowboys to run things in his absence?

Cody knew it was none of his business, but what in the world did that city slicker think she was going to do on Frank's ranch? Her clothes looked brand new yesterday. Her constant look of perplexity almost had him laugh aloud. She couldn't even water the horses without help.

He frowned. What happened to the power? He hadn't heard of any outages. But if it didn't affect the Rocking F, he wouldn't have heard. He hoped the generator ran until the power was restored.

Then he frowned again. Would she know how to shut it down and retap into the electrical power?

"Not that it's my problem," he said aloud. His horse twitched his ears hearing his voice.

"And what happened to Ed? Someone should be there to run things."

And not some slender brown-haired woman with wide gray eyes. He tried to remember her but drew a complete blank. Surely she visited her dad growing up. He knew the man was divorced, but nothing about the circumstances. Was there only the one child? Not a child any more. She was a fish out of water on a ranch.

Cody felt the growing heat of the day. He'd see what he could do about the Braddock cattle, then head in to get the truck and the wire. He'd thought he was done with that chore for a while.

He hoped Jarred hadn't assigned Jose something he couldn't break away from. Cody liked working with Jose. He didn't pontificate on what was wrong with ranching these days like Aaron did. Just because he was the oldest hand on the ranch didn't make his every statement gospel.

Why didn't he remember her? Surely Frank would have brought her over to see his parents at some point. He couldn't imagine not remembering her now. Pretty. He'd definitely describe her as a hot-house flower. How long it would take before she left? First time she got mud on her boots, he'd bet.

What could his grandfather tell him about Holly Braddock?

When he reached the breach in the fence, he scanned the area. Most of the cattle were still near the trees, some in the shade. He didn't see another horse but kept an eye out for others. Frank had to have more than two horses.

He circled the cattle, bunching them together and driving them toward the opening in the fence. They moved along with little protest, but he knew it would have been easier with one of their cattle dogs. That'd teach him to go looking for cattle without one. Maybe he'd bring one back when he came to fix the break.

It was high noon by the time Cody reached the ranch house. He unsaddled his horse and turned him loose in the corral and headed inside for something to eat. The house was empty. Washing up he made himself a couple of peanut butter and jelly sandwiches.

They seriously needed to do some shopping to replenish

the kitchen. He found milk in the refrigerator and downed a glass. What he wouldn't give for a big roast beef sandwich with lots of mustard. Finishing the second sandwich, he scrounged around for something else to eat.

Cookies would be good or some of his mother's pound cake. He'd even settle for an old candy bar. But the cupboards were practically empty.

He cleaned up and headed back out for the afternoon. His grandfather's truck was gone. He was most likely in town or visiting another ranch. Impatient to ask him about Frank's daughter, he considered for a moment taking off into town to see if he could find him. And maybe pay his respects to Frank. Would Holly be visiting her father now?

No, duty first. He needed to repair that fence.

He checked the truck for the supplies he'd need, then went to the bunk house to see if any of the hands were there eating lunch. Carlos was already at the stove preparing dinner. When asked, he said the others had packed a lunch that day and gone to work with Jarred.

Cody headed out alone, thinking about Holly Braddock and wondering if she would be able to manage on her own until her father recovered. Not that he cared either way.

3

Holly stopped for a large coffee before heading for the convalescent hospital. When she arrived at her father's room, there was someone sitting beside the bed, chatting.

"Hi," she said entering.

"Well, look at you. I bet Frank is thrilled to beat the band to see you're here," the man said with a broad smile.

Holly knew instantly he was related to Cody Fallon because of the deep blue eyes. Did everyone in that family have the same colored eyes?

"You know me?" she said.

"Holly. Frank talks about you all the time. And shows us pictures after every one of your visits. I know he'll be glad you're here."

Holly glanced at the bed. Her father appeared to be sleeping.

"He slept through my visit yesterday," she said, coming to stand beside the bed, gazing down at him. He looked so frail and pale. She wanted him back to normal. "The nurse said that was his body healing."

"Reckon so. I'm Seth Johnson from the Rocking F. Our ranch shares a boundary with the Braddock place."

"I met Cody a little while ago. He brought two horses in. They'd been running free and I guess that's not a good thing?"

"Hard on horses unless they're born wild. Those we've domesticated need a bit more care."

"He said they needed the farrier. Do you know who dad uses?"

"Randy Palmer as do we. Good man, in demand, though. I bet he has a standing schedule for your ranch. He does with ours."

"Were you and dad talking?" she asked.

"No, he's been asleep the whole time. I heard stroke victims can hear things, so I'm keeping him up to date on what's going on in Wildcat Creek."

Frank moved restlessly beneath the sheet.

The movement caught Holly's attention. She smiled when she saw her dad open his eyes. He looked confused for a moment, then settled on Holly, a smile turning up the corners of his mouth.

"H-h-h-aw—"

He frowned as the effort to speak.

"Hi Dad, I'm so glad to see you."

She gave him a hug and kiss on his cheek. Brushing back his hair she smiled at him through the tears gathering in her eyes.

"I was scared to death when I heard."

"H-h-hooowww—"

"I'll leave you two to talk," Seth said, reaching out to shake his friend's hand. "I'll be back tomorrow. You two have a good visit, now, ya hear? And you, Missy, you call on us if you need anything, anything a-tall."

"Thank you."

She watched Seth leave then drew the chair near the bed.

"I came as soon as I heard about the stroke. The doctor said yesterday you have a great shot at getting back to normal, it'll just take some work."

"M-m-m-oo der—"

"Do you mean mom? Yeah, as you guessed she had a hissy fit when I told her I was coming. She was sorry to hear of the stroke, but she didn't think I could do anything. But I know I can. I can help. Just let me know how."

She bit her lower lip, wondering if she should tell him Ed was gone. It looked to her like he was the only one working on the ranch. Still, if her father recovered soon, as the doctor suggested he could, it wouldn't be too long before he'd be back in charge. For all he'd done for her, she could keep it going until he was back.

"I took the room I used before," she said, not dwelling on the fact it had been ten years at least since she'd been on the ranch. The decorations were still suitable for a teenager.

"K-k-kat m-m-me hup," he said.

It tore at Holly's heart to hear him struggle so hard to speak. She hoped that part of the recovery happened by leaps and bounds. How frustrated he must be not to be able to communicate.

"Europe was fabulous. My favorite place was Rome. I spent almost three weeks there."

She had written him postcards from every location, her way to share some of the amazing sights she saw. She talked for a while on the benefits of train travel, how she coped with her rudimentary French, and the kindness of the people in the different countries.

When his eyes began to droop, she knew he was growing tired.

"I'll be back tomorrow," she said.

He shook his head, but she was firm.

"You need rest. And there are a few things I need to get before heading back to the ranch. I'll see you tomorrow."

Holly didn't burden her father with the situation at the ranch. He was doing more poorly than she expected. The last thing he needed was to worry about the ranch. He needed to focus on getting well, not on fretting about things he couldn't deal with yet.

She looked up the address of the power company and headed there once she left the convalescent hospital. There was a short line inside and she waited patiently. When her turn came, she stepped up to the counter.

"Hi, I'm Holly Braddock. I'm staying at the Bar-B-Bar ranch. The power is off and I'd like it turned back on," she said, conscious of others behind her in line.

She waited while the woman typed some information into the computer.

"That'll be $1,257.53."

"What?" Had she heard her wrong? "I don't understand."

"The billing is in arrears $1,257.53. Until it's paid in full, we don't turn on the power."

"That's can't be right."

"Four months in arrears. We sent notices. If you don't have the money, come back when you do. Until then, nothing changes."

Holly stepped away from the counter in shock.

She didn't have that money lying around. How could her father be in arrears? And for so long? Had he just forgotten to pay the bills?

She received a check every month, for more than the cost of the electric bill. How could he send her money and not pay his bills?

A sinking feeling dropped in her stomach.

Surely he didn't send her money and deny his own expenses.

She sat in her car for a long moment, unsure what to do. Finally, she called her mother.

"Hello?"

"Hi Mom, it's me."

"How is Frank?" she asked.

"Terrible. He looks like he's a hundred years old, lost weight and can't even talk."

Holly blotted the tears from her eyes.

"Mom, it would break your heart. I talked to a doctor yesterday and he said the outlook was good, but it'll be a slow recovery."

"I'm sorry to hear that. Is there anything you can do to aid that recovery?"

"Not really. Not that they said."

"Then you need to come home."

"I can't do that. I want to stay until he's better."

"You just said that will be a slow recovery. You have plans. What about that job offer you were considering when you took off for Wyoming? It won't stay available forever."

"I'm needed here, Mom."

"You just said you can't do anything to aid in his recovery."

"I know, but I can help around the ranch."

"Oh, that."

Holly knew her mother had grown to hate the ranch. She spoke often enough about it every time Holly had visited her dad. The comments had died down once she no longer made annual trips.

But Holly didn't see it in the same light as her mother. She had always loved her visits. And it felt right to be standing by her father now. He'd done a lot for her over the years. Though he couldn't be with her all the time, he still made sure she enjoyed all that life offered.

"I know you're not a fan of the ranch, Mom. But it's daddy's home and livelihood. Someone needs to see to it until he can again."

"Let one of those cowboys handle it. You need to get back home."

Holly shook her head, knowing her mother couldn't see her.

"Not yet," she said.

"Honestly, I don't know what you're thinking. Jobs like that one don't grown on trees."

"There'll be other jobs in the future, Mom. I'm needed here."

For the first time she could remember, she felt needed. She wanted to help her father.

"Good grief. I hope you come to your senses before too much longer. Call me when you do."

"Wait, mom, I need a favor."

"Such as?" her mother's voice sounded wary.

"I need some cash."

"Visit an ATM."

"More money than I can get from an ATM. And more than I have in my checking account anyway."

"How much and what for?"

"A thousand dollars." She had enough in her bank account to cover the difference. But she needed the thousand to pay off the electric bill."

"Good grief, whatever for? Ask your father."

"It's, um, to pay the electric bill. He was in arrears."

"To a thousand dollars worth?" her voice rose in confusion.

"I don't know what happened, but the power's off at the ranch and I don't have enough to pay it off the bill so I can get it turned back on."

"And Frank can't pay it?"

"I don't know. He can't even talk, so I doubt he can handle anything financial right now. And I don't have access to his bank account."

Her father would have enough in the bank to pay the bill. Yet if so, why hadn't he paid it?

"There's no electricity at the ranch?" her mother asked.

"Nope."

"So how are you managing?"

"I just got here yesterday, one night wasn't so bad. But I can't stay there if there's no electricity."

"Then come home."

"Mom! Please, just put the money in my account. I'll pay you back when I can."

"I'm not encouraging you to stay there. That ranch has been a money pit since the get go. I still remember your father putting cattle ahead of me. Maybe a few days without electricity will bring you to your senses. Come home before someone snaps up that job."

Holly gritted her teeth.

"Mom, I can get another job. I need help here."

"Get it from your father."

To Holly's astonishment, her mother hung up on her.

She knew her mother resented her father, always had as far back as Holly could remember. But she thought her mom would help her out.

Obviously she'd been wrong.

Gazing out the window, she wondered what she could do next? She thought about some of her friends. She didn't feel comfortable about asking any of them for such a big loan. Did she have anything she could sell?

Looking around the car, she knew she had to turn in the rental. If she had no money to turn on the electricity, she better be careful with her remaining money. With her father unable to access his bank account who knew when she'd get another check.

And who knew what other expenses might crop up.

She needed money for food and feed.

There was the truck at the ranch she could use, she'd parked next to it last night. The keys had to be around somewhere. Since her father had been taken to the hospital by ambulance, the keys were most likely still at the ranch.

Could she get a ride out there once she turned in the car? Time to find out.

She called the rental agency to find out about turning the car in without having to go the airport. There was a satellite office in Coleville.

There was a penalty for not returning it where she rented it, but the total cost would be far less than continuing to rent it for a week.

She drove to Coleville and found the gas station that acted as a satellite office and turned in the car. Walking out into the heat of the day, she considered all she needed doing if she was going to keep things going until her father was better.

First off, she needed to get a ride to the ranch and then find the truck keys.

She spun around and went back inside.

"Can you tell me where the feed store is?" she asked.

She figured that would be the best place to find a cowboy who might be heading back to Wildcat Creek.

Following the directions, she found it only a mile across town from the gas station. She hoped there would be someone who might give her a lift back to Wildcat Creek.

Asking at the counter, she was pleased to hear there was a rancher heading out in a few minutes who would pass right by the driveway to the Bar-B-Bar.

"Hi, I'm Kristi Donovan. I hear you need a ride back to Wildcat Creek."

Holly smiled at the friendly woman.

"I'd appreciate it. I just turned in my rental car and realized I have no way to get back home."

"And where's home?"

"Bar-B-Bar, for now," Holly said.

"I pass right by it on my way home. Glad to give you a lift. You related to Frank Braddock?"

"Yes, I'm his daughter."

Kristi chatted with Holly as they left Coleville. Holly knew the woman was curious about Frank's daughter that no one seemed to know about. Holly answered all her questions, but volunteered little beyond that.

In less than a half hour they reached the ranch and Kristi drove right up to the house.

She took a pad from her purse and wrote her phone number.

"Here, call if you want company or help or anything," she said offering Holly the paper.

"Thanks, I appreciate that. And thanks again for the ride."

Entering her dad's bedroom a short time later, Holly spotted the ring of keys on his dresser, along with his wallet, some loose change and a pair of pliers and two different screw drivers.

"Is that what a prepared rancher carries around?" she asked the empty room, noting the tools.

Taking a peek into his wallet it saddened her to see a total of eleven dollars. Her father had to have more money in his bank account. She'd have to see about getting access so she could buy the feed the horses needed.

And see about getting the power turned back on.

Carlos piled the platters high and handed them off to Felipe to put on the long table. The men were laughing at a joke Pedro told when Cody entered the bunkhouse. He was starving. He noted he was the last to arrive as he pulled out his chair and sat. In less than five minutes all had been served and there was a momentary lull in the conversation as the first pangs of hunger were assuaged.

"Find those cattle?" Jarred asked.

"Yep. Twenty head. Belonged to Bar-B-Bar. Drove them over and repaired the fence. A gate came down."

Cody didn't pause in his eating to fill them in.

"Horses, too, right?" Billy Bob asked.

"Yep, two of them. Didn't see a third."

"I saw Holly at the hospital today," Seth said, glancing between his grandsons.

"Holly?" Jarred asked.

"Frank's daughter," Cody replied before his grandfather could. "She was at the ranch when I brought the horses in. She's staying there, I guess until her father's better."

Jarred looked at his grandfather. "Do you know her?"

"I met her today, but I've seen her pictures over the years. Frank's really proud of her."

"What does she do?"

"I don't rightly know," Seth said. He looked down the table at Cody. "She tell you?"

Cody shook his head.

"How's Frank doing?" Cody asked. "I told his daughter I'd visit next time I'm in town."

"He's not doing so well, from the looks of it. He's stable and recovering, but looks sickly and he can't talk worth a plugged nickel. No telling how long before he's back in fighting form–if ever."

"Tough," Cody said. "Ed left."

"What?"

Everyone at the table looked at him.

"Who's taking care of the place?" Jarred asked.

"Don't know. That Holly, I guess."

Seth frowned. "She used to visit when she was younger but I don't believe she's been on the ranch in ten years. She can't know enough to keep it going until Frank's back."

Cody shrugged.

"She can hire someone. I'd like to know what Ed was thinking just turning the horses loose and taking off. I'd check the safe to make sure he didn't also abscond with funds."

Jarred nodded. "I'll put out some feelers, see if I can find out what happened, where he is now. Meantime, keep an eye on things for Frank, will you?"

"Why me?" Cody asked.

He didn't especially want to be around Frank's daughter. She was a looker, but too polished and rarefied for him. Plus he doubted she'd stick around for long. She looked too high maintenance to live on a working ranch. Especially one that looked as shabby as the Bar-B-Bar. It had surprised him to see how rundown it appeared when he showed up that morning.

"You know her," Jarred said.

"I spent about a half hour with her this morning, that's hardly knowing anyone," Cody argued. He looked down the table at Jarred. "You want her taken care of, you do it."

"Do you have to argue about everything?" Jarred asked.

Cody grinned. "Only with you, bro."

"I figured that," Jarred mumbled. "Blast it, someone needs to make sure Frank's animals aren't neglected. You wouldn't be a stranger showing up. She's met you. Just do it."

Cody leaned back in his chair and challenged his brother. "You can meet her."

Seth slapped his hand on the table.

"Someone take it on and watch out for the ranch. Whether she stays or goes, there's no one else there and the Bar-B-Bar has been our neighbor for as long as I can remember. Stop your bickering and watch out for the ranch."

Cody nodded. He may be reluctant to do anything Jarred suggested, but he wouldn't let any animal suffer. He'd be surprised if the hot-house daughter was there in a week. With Ed gone, there'd be a lot of work to do. Not that he planned to do it.

But he could help until they hired someone. Or a couple of someones.

Jarred frowned at him, but wisely said nothing with Seth glaring at both of them.

Cody knew he and his brother argued more than anyone, but sometimes Jarred's attitude rubbed him the wrong way. Make that most of the time. Older by eighteen months didn't give him special powers.

"I'll take it on, Grandpa," he said reluctantly, returning to his food. It was the neighborly thing to do.

Once dinner ended, Cody headed for his place.

The ranch held six cottages that offered accommodations for married ranch hands. When one had become available two years ago, Cody claimed it for his own. A living room, bath, small kitchen and one bedroom was all there was, but it was his domain and he could escape the rest of the family when he wanted some alone time.

He flung open the door, the heat of the day captured inside. Leaving the door open, he put on a fan, loathed to turn on the air conditioning before bed. The place would cool down enough to be tolerable in short order. He tossed his hat on the rack on the wall and flopped down on the sofa. Flicking on the television, he clicked through the stations until he found something worth watching.

But his mind was on the pretty woman he'd met that

morning. The soft hair that framed her face. The wide gray eyes that were so expressive. The startled look in her eyes when he told her about needing to go out to look for any other horses. She could ride, couldn't she?

Which horse could she ride? The gaunt one or the one with the gash on his flank?

"Blast it," he hadn't thought it through. Neither horse was up to work for a while. They both needed rest and feeding.

His grandfather was right, the animals needed care, not only those two horses, but any others on the ranch. And the water holes needed to be checked to make sure there was plenty of water in this heat. And if an animal was injured, quick treatment was important.

Cody had done a course in college on first aid for animals. He'd even toyed with the idea of becoming a vet at one time. But the varied tasks of ranching called for more than fixing hurt or sick animals. That's one aspect he really liked–the variety.

He'd ride over in the morning and take one of their horses. Holly couldn't weigh that much so any mount he took would do. Maybe Starlight. She was getting up there in years, still liked to run when given the command, but not as long on stamina as she'd once been.

He hoped to goodness that rancher's daughter could ride.

And the sooner they had someone there who knew what they were doing the better. He'd suggest she hired someone right away.

Cody took the long way around the next morning, leading Starlight. It was early enough that the sun was just peeping over the horizon. Which meant it was as cool as it would be that day. He followed the driveway up to the ranch house, checking the fence on either side. Built strong. It looked to be in good shape. No breaches here which would mean cattle on the road.

The driveway was rutted a little, nothing major, but should be smoothed out the next time the ground was soft enough. And a layer of gravel wouldn't hurt.

When he came closer to the house, the shabby shape it was in became clear. It should have been repainted years ago. With the old paint peeling, it'd be twice as much work to scrape and paint as it would have been to paint before it got so bad.

When he rounded the house he saw the corral. The horses were eating from the hay that had been tossed in for them. At least she'd followed through on that. He came up to the rails and dismounted, tying his horse and then leading Starlight to the rails and tying her. He'd make sure they both got water once he found Holly.

She came out of the barn just as he rounded his horse.

"Oh, I didn't expect to see you here," she said, halting.

Cody nodded a greeting. She wore the same jeans and boots from yesterday, but today's top was pink and pretty. Too fancy to be of much use on a working ranch. She pulled her hair back into a pony tail which emphasized the classic features of her face.

"I figured you could use some help rounding up the other horse. And those two aren't up to a day's work yet."

She looked at his two horses. "Thanks."

"You visit your father yesterday?" Cody asked.

She nodded.

"Did he say why Ed left?"

"I didn't bring it up. No sense worrying him about the ranch when he needs to focus on getting well. If I can just hold it together until he's better, I'll do it."

"Know much about ranching?" he asked.

She shook her head. "But I can learn."

He gave a half laugh of disbelief. "Yeah, right."

"Hey, you weren't born knowing how to do things, you learned."

"I've had almost thirty years of learning how to do things. You expect to pick it up in what, two days?"

"Well, then I can hire someone, like dad did. Only someone who will stay this time."

"Better plan. Right now let's look for any missing horses, I have other things to do today."

"You didn't have to come here. I can manage."

Cody shook his head in disbelief. She still looked like a woman dressed up to play cowgirl. Her boots were a bit more dusty than yesterday, but those jeans were almost indecent so dark and new looking. And by the tight way they fit her he wondered if she could even get a leg over a horse.

"Just being neighborly. Come on, daylight's burning."

She almost smiled at that. "My dad used to say that all the time when I visited as a kid."

Cody walked past her and into the barn. She turned round and followed him inside.

"What are you doing now?"

"Looking for a saddle for you. Starlight isn't an easy bareback ride."

"Starlight?"

"The horse I brought for you to use."

He entered the tack room and took a bridle from a peg. It would do. He turned to one of the saddled on the rack, but she stepped in first.

"I can manage," she said, reaching out to pull the saddle off the stand.

Cody turned to go back outside and heard a sound behind him. Looking back, he saw Holly sitting on the floor, the saddle in her lap, her legs splayed out in front of her.

"You can manage?" he said, raising an eyebrow.

It took all the manners his mother had drilled into him not to burst out laughing.

"It's heavier than I expected," she said in a haughty tone.

He reached out and snagged the saddle, slinging it over his shoulder and walking out to the horses. Yeah, right this woman could manage. At this rate, Frank should authorize the sale of the ranch and give up before anything worse happened than the horses turned loose.

Holly scrambled up and hurried after him.

"Just because it was unexpected doesn't mean I can't manage."

"You can ride, right?"

"Of course. I rode all the time when I came to visit my dad when I was a child."

"So who saddled your horse then?"

"My dad. I was just a kid."

"Ummm. Why did you stop coming?"

"What?"

"When was the last time you were here and why did you

stop coming to visit. I've known Frank all my life, he and my dad are friends. But I don't remember you."

Cody made quick work of saddling the horse. He looked at her legs, gauging how long to make the stirrups, then unhitched the horse and handed the reins to her. He was curious to see what she'd do next. Especially how those tight jeans would work mounting a horse.

She took the reins and went to the left side of the horse. Nothing happened. He looked over the horse. She was looking around the yard.

"Problem?"

"It's high. Isn't there a mounting block or something?"

He looked away in disgust.

"This isn't some fancy riding academy. If you can't get on here without, what would you do out on the range if you get off and need to get back on."

"I wouldn't get off," she said. "Can't we drive the horses in without getting off?"

"Who knows. Anyway, use the fence rail. And let's get going."

He snapped the reins from the fence and mounted his horse in one smooth motion. Setting his hat more firmly on his head, he watched as she led the horse to the corral fence and scrambled on to the saddle. It took a couple of seconds for her feet to find the stirrups.

"Where's your hat?' he asked.

"I don't have one. I'll be okay."

"Your face will burn off if you don't watch it. This sun is nothing to mess with."

He urged his horse closer to hers and took off his own hat, and handed it to her.

"What about you?" she asked, holding the hat awkwardly.
"I'll manage. Let's go."

Cody headed out of the ranch yard and out to the pasture that adjoined the Rocking F. He didn't wait to see if she followed. She either could ride well enough to keep up or not. But he wasn't going to slow down for her. He had chores around the Rocking F to see to, he couldn't spend all day on searching for missing Bar-B-Bar horses.

Holly put the hat on. It fell to her ears. She pushed it back a little and kicked the horse. Cody was already several yards ahead of her. She had mixed emotions about his showing up. On the one hand, she welcomed his help. She hadn't a clue how to find the horses or get them back to the corral.

Yet his attitude annoyed her. No one asked him to come help. If he showed up on his own the least he could do is be gracious about it.

She feared what he'd said earlier would be true. He'd spent his entire life learning the ranching business. She had a dozen summers of visiting when she was younger. Then her interests had changed and time slipped away. Before she knew it, it had been ten years since she'd visited.

It wasn't all her fault, she defended herself. Her father had flown to Palm Springs to see her. Some times taking her to Disneyland or San Francisco. Once arranging a great visit in New York City and another year in Washington D.C. He hadn't expected her to take over the ranch.

Had he?

She gazed around the land they were riding over. In the distance the silhouette of the mountains showed hazy blue. The rolling hills between seemed to go on forever. Trees dotted the landscape here and there, providing some welcomed shade in the heat of the day. Small groups of cattle grazed on the brown grass or lay beneath one of the trees.

Holly was glad to be back. How proud she'd been when her father let her ride around with him. It was hard to say she recognized anything as it looked all the same to her. The same as it had when she was riding with her dad and soaking up every word he said about cattle and feed and weather.

The sun was growing hotter. She was glad to have Cody's hat, but her arms were beginning to burn. She should have worn a long sleeve shirt as he had. She'd have to return home before too much longer if she didn't want a bad sunburn.

Holly was about to say something to him when he pulled to a stop and pointed toward the left. "There are two more. How many did your dad have?"

"I have no idea," she said, barely making out the horses in the distance. She could see a bunch of animals but they all looked like cattle to her. Wait, there was a horse. How had he seen them to begin with?

"Can we find that Ed guy and ask him?" she asked.

"Or ask your dad."

"I don't want to worry him and letting him know the horses were loose would start that. He needs to focus on getting well."

"Suit yourself," Cody said.

In less than five minutes they approached the two horses. One was grazing the other watched as they approached. Holly had never seen these horses before. The one she'd ridden as a child had been sold long ago. It had been too small for most ranch work, but perfect for a little girl who liked to visit and pretend she lived in Wyoming.

How different would her life be if she had stayed longer with her father or even come to live with him as a teenager?

She glanced at the cowboy beside her. They'd know each other if she'd lived here. He was older by a few years, but since her father and his were friends, they would have known each other.

What was he like? How did he enjoy living on ranch? Did he yearn to see more of the world?

The past was what it was. She stopped the horse, already feeling her muscles begin to grow stiff. She was so not used to riding and knew she'd regret this later.

But die before she'd confess that to Cody Fallon.

"Easy. Don't want to spook them," he murmured, riding toward the one watching them.

"Easy, fellow," he crooned.

The horse looked at Cody and then at Holly but didn't move.

"A good sign," Cody whispered.

He drew the lariat from his saddle and shook out the loop on the side away from the horse so not to startle him.

He sidled closer until he could toss the loop over the horse's head. The horse danced a little sideways, but didn't run.

"Let's see if the other one will follow," he said to Holly.

He held out the end of the rope.

"Wrap the end around your saddle horn and start back. I'll get behind this other one and see if he'll stop eating long enough to move."

Holly hoped she could remember the way back. Everything looked the same to her. She didn't want to make a fool of herself. She got that he didn't think highly of her.

Fortunately, Starlight seemed to know the way, though Holly was afraid at first the horse would head back to the Rocking F ranch. But she saw some hoof prints in the dust and knew they were retracing their steps.

She heard the others behind her.

It was slow going but they finally reached the corral, Cody opened the gate, and took the rope from her to loosen it from the horse's neck. Both horses ambled in and headed for the water tank.

"Good job," he said, coiling the rope and tying it on his saddle. "They need food."

"Of course. I didn't see any other horses."

Holly wasn't sure she could get off this horse by herself. But she refused to ask for help.

The casually given compliment warmed her heart. She couldn't follow that with a show of weakness. Not if she wanted the respect of this cowboy neighbor.

Fortunately, he dismounted and walked into the barn, affording her a moment of privacy. She flung her leg over, kicked the other stirrup free and slid to the ground. She held on to the horse's mane or she would have collapsed in the dirt. Her knees felt as weak as soggy spaghetti noodles. Locking them, she limped to the corral fence and tied Starlight. She patted the horse's neck.

"Thanks for the ride," she whispered.

Cody came out and tossed over a couple of flakes of hay.

"I could have done that," she protested, not wanting him to know how weak her legs felt.

She needed to get in better shape.

"No problem. You going out again to look for any other horses?"

His face looked browner than earlier. She took off his hat and handed it to him, shaking her head.

"Maybe later. I need to see if I can find Ed or someone else who knows something about the ranch. There may not be others or there could be half dozen out there somewhere."

"Try the feed and grain to find Ed. It acts as a clearing house sometimes for ranch hands changing jobs."

He reached out and touched her arm lightly.

"Better get something on that. And next time wear a hat and long sleeves. You might invest in some leather gloves, too."

Holly looked at her hands. Her bright red polish had chipped and she'd broken a nail and never noticed. She curled her hands into fists and hid them against her side.

"Okay. Thanks again for your help."

"You okay unsaddling Starlight?"

"You're not taking her home?"

"No, she's for you to use until your own horses gain some weight and build back their stamina."

She longed to ask him to unsaddle the horse so she didn't have to move a muscle. But pride kept the words back.

"I'll manage. I can get the saddle off even if it's hard to swing up that high. You must have things to do at your place."

"I do, but not as much as it seems here."

"I'll go into town this afternoon and see about hiring some help."

Though how she'd go about that was beyond her. She hadn't a clue what questions to ask someone applying to work on a ranch.

That they know how to saddle a horse would be number one.

Cody took off for home, the situation at the Bar-B-Bar nagging at him. He knew full well that hot-house flower couldn't manage the ranch.

But he recognized pride when he saw it. He'd give her a chance to find a solution. Then if none appeared, he'd see what he could do.

It would help if her father was able to deal with things even if from a hospital bed. But it sounded to him like Frank had his hands full just recovering from the stroke.

Man, he hoped he never had a stroke. He'd hate to be helpless, not able to talk. Dependent on others for food and care.

Shaking off the gloom, he put Smoke to a lope, the sooner to get home, get some grub, and do his own chores.

5

"I will not panic," Holly told herself again.

She took a deep breath and held it before letting it out. The news at the feed and grain had been bad enough yesterday when they wouldn't extend her any credit because of the balance on the account. She'd used her credit card to get enough grain to feed the horses.

Now they wouldn't even post the job for her because of Ed lodging a complaint that he hadn't been paid for two months. He was working at another ranch in the area. She got his contact information and was stunned by what he told her. Her father was close to bankruptcy.

And she hadn't a clue.

The realization of the cost of her trip to Europe swept over her. She'd spared no expense. It was costly in London and Paris, but she'd indulged herself, using the credit card her father paid for. Indulging herself whatever the whim.

She felt sick. Sick and afraid. She'd thought her father had plenty of money. He'd never once in all her life said anything about watching expenses.

She'd caused this. She'd been indulged far beyond what she should have been. Was it to prove to her mother he could provide for their child in the manner in which her mother thought appropriate?

A myriad of expenditures played through her mind. The car she'd bought when she graduated high school. The trip to New York with all the plays they'd seen. Just the allowance he provided when she should have been working her way through college and then getting a job. Why had she thought she got a free ride through life?

She couldn't tell her mother. She harped enough on the lifestyle she'd shared with Holly's father. Holly refused to add any fodder to her criticism.

Now her father was lying gravely ill. She didn't want to question him for fear of adding to his worries. She realized he must be worried sick knowing the state of his finances and his inability to work to get through the morass.

Did he know Ed had left? Maybe he thought the cowboy was still holding the ranch together. She wished she knew when Ed had left. She should have asked when she had him on the phone.

There had to be something she could do to make things right.

Cody Fallon had stated it that morning, she knew nothing about running a ranch. But she knew about business. She had a blasted degree in fine arts, but had taken some basic business courses thinking she'd work in a museum and need to have a working knowledge of non-profits. Time she applied that knowledge to something practical.

Think!

Ideas popped. She withdrew her iPad and started a list. The first thing was to see if she could get power of attorney from her father.

Assess where he stood financially.

Start a strategic plan for pulling out of the red.

Cut any expense that didn't contribute to the bottom line.

See if she could raise some money.

If she could get a loan to get started, that would help.

If not, she could sell her car. But beyond that, she had no access to any substantial amount of money—certainly not enough to pay Ed and get food for the horses or hire another hand to help with the cattle.

The threatening panic subsided as she assessed what she could do and what she needed help with.

The first order of business—get power of attorney from her father.

Holly ate dinner in town. She couldn't face eating granola bars and bottle water at the ranch and with the power still off, she couldn't use the refrigerator for any other food. She bought bread, peanut butter, jelly, packaged cookies and more granola bars. Until she got things going, that electric bill was impossible to deal with.

And the generator had run out of gas yesterday afternoon.

She'd found an attorney in the phone book and when she called, found he knew her father and could draw up the power of attorney—as long as he received confirmation from Frank Braddock's doctor that even if he couldn't talk, Frank could understand and decide to grant his daughter power of attorney.

Holly had then gone to see her father.

She knew from his agitation that he didn't like the idea, but she stood by her request, telling her father it was the only way to make sure the ranch didn't fail until he was better. Finally, he agreed to her request.

Holly suspected he didn't want her aware of the extent of debt, but she felt so guilty about spending money so freely her whole life, she was doubly intent on bringing the ranch out of the red.

Her heart ached for the years she'd seen her father so little. For the lonely life he'd had while she'd been off doing whatever she wanted and spending his money like it was water.

Guilt swept through her. She would make it right no matter what!

She finished her dinner, lingering a little over the hot coffee. It might be her last until the next time she came to town.

Which she hoped was tomorrow with news from the attorney the paperwork was complete. Extremely aware of the cost of things, she wouldn't be driving in whenever the whim struck. She needed to make every trip count to conserve on gas.

Jotting more notes on things to look into, she wondered if she could possibly find a ranch hand who hadn't heard of their financial trouble and would give her a couple of weeks of work until payday. She knew she could get some money by then. Her mother could sell her car for her. That would bring in some working capital.

When she arrived back at the ranch, she could scarcely get out of the truck. Her hips ached, her calf muscles hurt, her thighs felt tight. Her arms burned. She felt as stiff as a ninety-two year old. And there were still the horses to see to.

She had a gas can in the back, hoping gas was all the generator needed to get going. It had stopped that first night and nothing she'd tried got it going again. The man in the feed and grain had told her how to fill it and how to start it. She needed the well to pump more water for the horses. And she wouldn't mind water in the house for a little while.

Following the instructions, she filled up the generator, then pulled the cord. Nothing. She tried again. The man had said to pull fast. It was hard, she could barely get it out. Bracing herself, she yanked for all she was worth and it roared into life.

Feeling proud of herself when the generator kicked in, she knew it was a small thing. Small steps were all she could manage right now.

By the time she fed the horses and filled the water trough, Holly could scarcely stand. She'd give anything for a soaking in a hot bath, but the water heater didn't seem connected to the generator, so another cold spit bath would be all she could muster.

She crashed into bed before eight o'clock, tired and achy and was asleep in seconds.

Cody sat on the wide porch of the family home, tilted back in a chair, his boots resting on the railing in front of him. It was quiet in the twilight. Once in a while a steer bellowed in the distance.

His grandfather sat in the rocker nearby, creaking as he moved back and forth.

Jarred was in the office. He'd volunteered to handle the

books while his parents were gone and Cody was happy to leave it to him. He liked the outdoor part of ranching, not so much the bookkeeping.

Kyle was out somewhere. That man kept to himself more than any of the brothers.

Many nights Cody sat on the front porch with his mom and dad and grandfather and usually Jarred and Ty, when he was home. He liked the peace at the end of the day.

"You help that Braddock girl today?" Seth asked after a while.

Twilight was giving way to dark. Stars began to sprinkle the skies.

"I did," Cody responded. "She'll never last."

"Maybe. Maybe not. Still, up to us to help."

"Us?" Cody said sardonically.

He hadn't seen anyone else from the ranch over there helping.

"You. You've the time and the know-how. Doesn't hurt to be neighborly."

"Not sure it helps," he said. "It'll only be staving off the inevitable if Frank doesn't get one hundred percent recovered. And it sounds like that's never going to happen."

"We don't now that. I'm going under the assumption he'll be back in a few months raring to go. Up to us to make sure we keep his place going until then."

"Grandpa, have you been over there lately? The corral fence looks like one rub by of a horse will knock it over. The house looks like it's falling down around them. The yard is as dusty as the dust bowl and there's hardly any hay in the barn. Those horses I saw will not be fit to work for a few weeks—as long as it takes to get them fattened up and their stamina builds." Cody shook his head. "It's a wreck."

"All the more reason that little gal needs help. Why are you so reluctant?"

"Hey, it's not my place. Why me? Talk to Jarred or Kyle. Maybe Ty will stop rodeoing and help some."

"Why not you?"

Cody thought about it. He was as interested in helping a neighbor as the next guy. That's what people did around here. Grandpa was right, though. He was resistant. More so than if it had been Frank asking.

It was Holly.

He didn't want to deal with her.

Because she wouldn't stay.

Dumb reason.

Because–she didn't know enough.

He did.

He scowled.

Because she looked like she should be in some fancy penthouse apartment, sipping champagne and not slogging through the dust and heat of Wyoming.

Because she was pretty enough to wrap a man's heart around her little finger, and then flit away like she'd never been here at all.

He rocked all four legs of the chair down on the porch and stood.

"I'm heading to bed. I'll ride over again tomorrow to see how the ranch is fairing. I hope she found the other horses."

"How many did you find?'

"Four so far."

"How many are still missing?"

"Don't know," Cody said. "I'm not sure how many Frank has. I haven't been to his place in years. I told you it needs a lot of work. The paint on the house and barn is peeling, lots of weathered wood showing. Why doesn't a man keep up his place?"

"There's been a recession."

"Hmm, yeah, but we keep our place up."

"Having oil on the property doesn't hurt. Your father's an excellent manager and he raised you boys up right, too. It takes a lot of teamwork to pull together. That's something we have. Even your uncle Jack would come over to help if needed."

"So much for Frank's team. His sole ranch hand up and left," Cody said.

Seth nodded. "Wondered about that. Used to be there were a half dozen men over there. One man can't run that ranch."

"Nor can one woman, especially if she hasn't a clue what's needed or how to do it. Her best bet is to hire a manager to run it until her father gets well."

Seth nodded. "Think on how to help her," he said to his grandson. "If only vetting a ranch hand."

"She'd likely hire the first guy who shows up in a cowboy hat and boots."

"So watch out for her," Seth said.

"Yeah, I know, it's the Fallon way."

Cody stepped down the shallow steps to the crushed shell walk way his mother liked so much. Crunching with each step, he headed for his place. He'd step up no matter how reluctant he felt. Grandpa was right, his father had raised his boys to help out neighbors, no matter who they were.

Cody entered the bunk house the next morning and headed straight for the coffee. He nodded to the others already sitting around the table, eating the big breakfast Carlos had prepared, eggs and grits, bacon and ham, biscuits and gravy and lots of coffee. Couldn't beat one of Carlos' breakfasts. It fueled a man for the day.

He grabbed a plate and dug in.

Jarred looked up. "I wanted to check out the pump on the far field. The one near Garrett's place. Felipe said it was making a funny noise. Can you help?"

"Going to Braddock's," Cody said, not pausing in eating.

"What for?"

"Ask grandpa."

Jarred's lips thinned.

"You're needed here."

Cody took a long pull from his coffee mug and looked at Jarred.

"Braddock's place is in bad shape and Grandpa wants one of us to look into it. You want to go?"

Jarred shook his head. "How long will you be?"

"Don't know. Depends on what needs doing."

Jarred had heard at dinner last night that there were no ranch hands on the Bar-B-Bar, only a girl from California who knew nothing about ranching.

"What needs doing?" he asked.

"I want to check on the horses that I brought in from the range, find out if there are any more missing. Then who knows what doesn't needs doing. I can get her to ride the fence, but if there's breach somewhere, she sure to goodness can't fix it."

"Send Pedro."

"Nope, they're our neighbors, we'll help out," Cody said.

His grandfather beamed proudly at him. Of course he knew Cody was only saying it to goad his brother. But what the hey.

"I'm heading for Abilene to check out that bull Dad wanted," Jarred said.

"Then let Kyle do it. He's handy with machines. He can figure out if we can fix it or need to call in the oil company."

Jarred looked around the table.

"And where is Kyle?"

"He rode out early, boss," Carlos said, piling another platter full of hot biscuits on the table. "Said he was gonna be gone all day. Took a lunch."

"Over to you, then Cody. When your babysitting at the Bar-B-Bar is done."

Cody nodded. "Shouldn't take all day. I'll go later."

The one thing about a ranch, there was never any down time.

When Cody rode up the drive to the Bar-B-Bar, he noticed again how shabby the house and barn looked. It would take a lot of work to get them back to the way he remembered from when he was younger. Stopping by the corral, he was pleased to notice all the horses had been fed and the water tank was full.

The rental car was gone. So was Frank's truck. Had Holly traded in her fancy rental car for the ranch truck? That'd surprise him. He'd have thought she wouldn't have touched the dusty old truck, much less drive it.

Starlight came to the fence ears forward. He urged Smoke closer so he could scratch her by her ears.

"Not working today, huh, girl? Where's Miss Holly?"

The horse nodded and then pulled back, going to the tank and taking a long drink.

"Unless I want to ride the ranch all day, I'm not needed here."

He dismounted and tied his horse to the corral fence. Walking into the barn, he checked out the food supply. The hay was going down as expected. He guessed there was enough for another three weeks. She'd need to restock before then.

Checking the grain bin, he was disappointed to see how little was there. Maybe she'd taken the truck into town today to get more. Her little car wouldn't have been suitable for hauling supplies.

Maybe she had the makings of a rancher after all. Time would tell.

He went back to his horse and mounted up. He'd check on the pump and then call back to see if Holly had returned. No sense riding over again if she wasn't home.

Holly sat opposite the banker and tried to hold back the tears. Her father had a hundred and seven dollars and seventeen cents in his bank account. And bounced check charges the bank was waiving because of his stroke.

She cleared her throat, stunned by the news.

"Ummm when does he get a deposit?" she asked.

"I don't understand?" the banker said.

He'd been kind all through the interview, while her own face burned with embarrassment. She trusted his discretion, but how long before the entire town knew the situation? Especially since Ed hadn't been very discreet.

"Doesn't he have any money coming in on a monthly basis or something?"

"From where? He's a rancher. Until he sells cattle there's no income."

"So if I sell some cows, I would have some money?"

He nodded.

She tried to smile but felt her lips begin to tremble.

Clearing her throat again she asked, "How do I sell cattle?"

"Find a buyer, arrange the deal. I could have one of the men here help you with that if you like. Or get someone knowledgeable with prices and buyers and more than I know about it to help you out. Check at the feed and grain. One of the men over there would know."

"Thank you. I'll have some money transferred in as soon as I can sell my car," she said.

"You are a signatory on the account now, so you'll be all set. I'm so sorry about your father. Frank's a good man. I hope he makes a complete recovery."

Holly walked slowly back to the truck. She'd eat lunch, call her mother to have her sell her car, and then head back to the ranch.

The car was several years old and Holly didn't have a clue how much she'd get for it. No matter how much, she knew it would be a drop in the bucket to what she needed. And kind as the banker had been, he had gently told her she wouldn't qualify for a loan. She had no work history, no collateral, and wasn't even known around town.

Another notch against her not visiting more often. If she had, maybe she'd have better resources. Friends willing to help.

Or she would have learned of the difficulties earlier and been better prepared to argue with her father when he wanted to spend money he really didn't have.

The phone call to her mother did not go well. Adrienne refused to sell Holly's car, saying she needed to leave the ranch and get back where she belonged.

"I'm needed here, mom. And if you won't lend me the money I need, I'll get it another way."

"By selling all you have, which isn't that much I might add. Just like your father to run the ranch into the ground without a care in the world of what would happen to you if he lost it."

"He's not going to lose it, Mom. I'll keep it going until he's better."

"Who's paying the medical insurance? I bet he let that lapse as well. You best look into selling the ranch and getting as much as you can for it. The longer you delay, the less it will be worth."

"Mom, try to understand. This is daddy's ranch. His reason for living. If I sell it, he has nothing."

"It sounds as if he's going to have nothing pretty soon anyway. Don't throw away your own life on a money-pit like that ranch. I remember when I wanted some new clothes, Frank argued what I had was fine and we needed the money for feed. Honestly, can't cows eat grass?"

Holly couldn't discuss that with her mother. She didn't know enough herself to answer that. She always thought ranch animals ate grass, but the horses needed more. Did cattle?

"If you won't help, then I'll find someone who can," Holly said finally.

She didn't want to spend the entire afternoon arguing with her mother.

"Honey, I'm doing this for you. There's no point in throwing good money after bad. You need to get home and start your job. If you delay, you'll lose it and the economy isn't that great that you'll find another one right away. If the money isn't coming from your father again, I don't know what we'll do."

"He's paid my trip to Europe," Holly said slowly.

"And he's been good about child support all along. I will give him that," Adrienne said.

"What do you mean all along?"

"Until lately. He's missed a payment or two."

"Mom, I'm way over eighteen. That's all he was required to pay–until I turned eighteen."

"Well he continued and I wasn't going to stop him."

Holly wanted to reach through the line and shake her mother. It wasn't only the trip to Europe she already felt guilty about, it was the months and years he didn't have to pay that he'd continued. And her mother hadn't told her.

Holly never considered her dad was continuing child support beyond what was required by law. She'd never thought about how much money her mother must make at the dress shop she worked in. She always had the latest in clothes, money enough to visit Las Vegas from time to time. Nice trips to Lake Tahoe.

"Mom, did you save any of that money? I really could use some now."

"Of course not, Holly. We spent every dime."

You did, Holly thought.

We did, she amended, feeling sick at heart. How could she have never inquired further into their financial situation?

It went back to thinking her father the most wonderful man in the world, and rich as could be, because he owned acres of land. Hadn't she heard the land rich, cash poor refrain before? She'd never applied it to her father.

"Okay, mom, if you won't help, then I won't keep you on the phone. I'll ask Brit to come get my car."

"Don't be foolish, Holly. Whatever you can get for a five year old car won't put a dent into operations of a cattle ranch."

"It might put a dent into it," she murmured then gave her mom a quick goodbye and pushed the disconnect button.

"I'm hoping it's enough to get the power back on and some food for the horses. And hire a man for a couple of weeks, until I can sell some of the cattle," she murmured feeling overwhelmed and alone. There was so much she didn't know.

The only thing she did know for sure was she'd do all she could to keep the ranch for her father. He'd cared for her beyond what she ever knew before. She would prove the investment worth it. She refused to let him lose his ranch!

5

Cody listened to the recording saying the phone had been disconnected. He hung up, frowning. Would the phone company do that merely because Frank was in the hospital? He didn't know, but it was inconvenient. Instead of calling to see if Holly was there, he'd have to go over and find out for himself.

He'd found Kyle earlier and the two of them had repaired the oil pump Jarred talked about. Kyle was hunting a wild cat and hadn't liked being pulled away from the hunt. The Rocking F hadn't lost any cattle to a mountain lion, but the Garrett ranch had and Kyle was hunting any sign the animal might be on their land.

Once finished with the repair, which did not need any more expertise than Kyle and Cody had between them, he resumed the hunt.

Cody cleaned up, grabbed lunch and tried the phone.

He debated riding over, but it was too hot to do a fence check or look for more horses. He'd take one of the trucks. If she wasn't home, he'd leave her a note this time.

Luck was with him, Frank's truck was parked near the barn. Holly had to be around somewhere.

She didn't come out when he stopped the truck. Surely she heard him arrive. He checked the barn first, but didn't see her. Heading toward the house, he instinctively went to the back door. It was closest and the one most likely used by family and friends.

The wooden door was wide open, only a screen door guarded the entry. Knocking he waited. No response.

"Holly?" he called.

She appeared a moment later.

"Cody? What are you doing here?"

She crossed the kitchen floor and pushed open the screen door and stepped outside.

She'd changed new jeans for shorts. Her feet were bare, her toes sparkling with some polish. He let his gaze drift down and back up.

He thought she should go back in and get into jeans before he swallowed his tongue.

"Well?" she asked, looking beyond him to his truck.

"I came to see if you need any help."

He looked closely. Her eyes were a bit red and puffy.

"Has something happened to Frank?" he asked.

She shook her head. "No, why?"

"You look like you've been crying."

She looked away an expression of annoyance on her face.

"I'm fine. Just sad my dad's so sick."

"Yeah, we are, too. So have you given any thought to hiring someone to help out?"

"Yes. I'll do that soon."

"Soon? Why not today? You went into town, right?"

"I had other things to see to," she said primly. "I'll get to hiring someone soon."

"And in the meantime?"

"What?"

"Who do you plan to look for those other horses? To check the cattle, check the fences, move cattle from one pasture to another if they've grazed it down, check the water holes and windmills–"

"Okay, okay, you've made your point. I'll see to it. Thank you for checking on me, but I think I'll be able to manage now."

"Your phone's out," Cody said.

"Is it? I've been using my cell."

"You get service out here?"

She shook her head.

"I make calls from town."

"You should get the phone reconnected. You'll need it in case of an emergency."

"I'll do that."

"Soon," he said.

She nodded. "Soon."

Cody studied her for a long moment. Something was off, but he couldn't tell what. Still, it wasn't his business if she rejected his help.

"Okay, then, I'll take off. Let me know if you need anything. I can help interview the cowboys if you like."

"We'll see. Thanks again for all your help."

"Hey, my dad and yours are friends. If he were here, he'd be helping as much as possible. That's what friends do."

She nodded.

"See you around," she said, and turned to reenter the house.

Cody ambled to the truck. Time he paid a visit to Frank Braddock. Maybe he knew what was going on.

At dinner that night, Seth suggested they invite Holly over for dinner on Sunday. Carlos didn't cook that night, so the Fallon men all chipped in and cooked with their mom away. Usually a big roast or spaghetti or sometimes they called into town for pizza and bought a half dozen pies to share.

Jarred looked at his grandfather. "Any reason why?"

"To be neighborly."

"Isn't Cody helping out neighborly enough?" Jarred asked glancing at his brother.

Cody looked over at his brother.

"Any reason why not?" he asked.

Jarred looked from his grandfather to his brother and shrugged.

"Just wondered. We haven't had Frank over in months even before mom and dad left on their cruise."

"He stopped coming when invited, but he is always welcomed, same as any neighbor," Seth said.

Jarred thought about it for a moment then nodded.

"I'd be interested in meeting his daughter. Is she pretty?" he asked Cody.

"Yes. And as out of place around here as an orchid would be."

"Maybe we should invite her soon, before she leaves, then," Jarred said. "Can you invite her, Cody?'

"Sure."

He wasn't going to tell everyone the phone was out of service. He'd drive over this evening and ask her. He wanted to talk to her about her father.

Cody had been shocked at the frailty of Frank Braddock. And dismayed to discover how little he could communicate.

He could almost feel the frustration Frank felt when he tried to talk. Little by little Cody began to ask yes-no questions to which Frank could respond better. He still wasn't clear on the entire situation, but he knew now Frank's situation was more dire than anyone else realized.

He wished he could talk with his father. But his parents only called in when in port. He wasn't sure when the next stop would be. Maybe he'd discuss things with his grandfather later. After he'd seen Holly.

In the meantime, he'd go along with anything Seth or Jarred suggested, to keep things quiet until he learned the extent of the problems at the Bar-B-Bar.

It was after dark by the time Cody drove into the yard at the Bar-B-Bar. His headlights picked out the horses in the corral, two of them ambling over to the fence to see the newcomer. The house was dark. Was Holly gone?

No, the truck was there.

It wasn't even eight o'clock yet. Had she gone to bed already?

Holly came out of the back door, the screen slamming behind her.

"What do you want now?" she asked walking over to the truck.

Cody looked behind her at the house. Why didn't he see any lights?

"I came by to invite you to dinner Sunday. If you're still here."

"Why wouldn't I be?" she asked, coming up to the truck.

"If you hire a manager, you can take off," he said.

"I'm here until my dad doesn't need me any more. And

that doesn't look like any time soon. Thanks for the invitation. How do I get to your place?"

"Turn left when you hit the highway and drive 4 miles. The driveway's marked. On the left."

"Okay. Shall I bring anything?"

"Nope, just an appetite."

She gave a half smile. "Count on it."

"Are you sitting in the dark?" he asked.

"No, I'm standing here talking with you."

He beat a rhythm on the steering wheel.

"You weren't when I drove up."

She shrugged and looked back toward the house.

"Power's out and I turned off the generator to conserve gas."

"How long before the electric company said it would be back on?" he asked.

The generator was good for some things, but it was a temporary fix at best.

"Did a transformer or something blow?" he asked.

"No and it'll be soon."

He looked at her.

"That seems to be your answer to everything. What happens soon."

She shrugged again.

"Holly."

She looked at him.

"What?"

"What's going on."

"Nothing that concerns you. I'm managing."

"I was in to see your dad today," Cody said.

"That was nice of you."

"Uh huh, and he confirmed there are only four horses, so you don't have to ride out to look for others."

"That's good. I don't think I can get that saddle on the horse's back."

"But there's fencing to check, water holes—"

"I know, I know. You went through everything before. I'll find a way."

Cody might not be the most intuitive individual around, but even he could tell something was off. He opened the door of the truck forcing Holly to take a couple of steps back.

"I'm fine, you can go home," she said, a hint of panic in her voice.

"Something's up and I'm staying until I find out what. In the meantime, I'll check the generator. You need lights at night. And water. What are you doing about the well?"

"The generator powers the well and the horses are taken care of."

"I can see that, what about you?"

She stared at him for a moment, then shocked him when her eyes filled with tears. Oh, Lord, deliver him from a woman crying.

"Don't cry," he said desperately.

"I'm not," she said turning away. A sob sounded.

"Oh, blast it," he said, running his hand around the back of his neck.

His grandfather should have come. He had more experience being married to his grandmother for forty three years before she died.

"Go home, Cody," she said, starting to walk to the house.

It was an out. He could take it as an order.

But his mother would skin him alive if he did.

Sighing, he followed her, reaching the back door at the same moment she did.

He touched her shoulder and she turned. In the faint light he could see tears on her cheek.

"Oh, Holly, it's going to be okay," he said, pulling her into a gentle hug.

It was as if he released a dam. She grabbed a fistful of his shirt, rested her head on his chest and bawled like a newborn.

Cody didn't know what to do. He was one of four boys in the family. None of them had a steady girlfriend at the moment. He hadn't a clue how to handle this situation. He tentatively rubbed her back, making soothing sounds like he'd gentle a scared puppy. He was so out of his league. If the phone had been working he could have called from home. He should have insisted his grandfather extend the invitation or Jarred or even Pedro.

"S-s-sorry," she said a moment later, turning and hurrying into the house.

One minute there, the next gone. He stood on the stoop for a moment, then took a deep breath and opened the door.

The house was hot and muggy. It was cooler outside. There was a single candle on the table, providing scant light. But he could make out the table and chairs, the refrigerator and stove. He listened carefully. She'd moved into the center of the house.

Should he leave? Or stay.

Not one to give up, Cody pulled out a chair and sat. He'd wait her out. Sooner or later, she'd be back. He just hoped it wasn't in the morning.

Five minute later Holly came back into the kitchen, carefully carrying another candle. She set it on the table and then saw Cody.

"Oh, I thought you left."

"Not until I find out what's going on," he said, pushing the brim of his hat back so he could see her better in the faint light.

Her eyes were definitely swollen. Probably red, but in this light everything looked sort of gray.

She pulled out a chair and sat.

"Just everything that could go wrong has. I never expected my dad to get sick. What if he doesn't recover? What if he's bedridden the rest of his life?"

Tears spilled over again.

"Yeah, but that's not what the doctor said. Without violating confidentiality he told me the prognosis looked good. That means he will get better," Cody countered.

She traced a pattern on the worn table.

"That's what he told me, too. But better from where he stands today doesn't necessarily mean a complete recovery. He could be wheel-chair bound, or never talk again. How will he run a ranch if he's not fit?"

"I thought you were going to take care of that," Cody said.

She gave a short laugh.

"Yeah, right. You know how prepared I am to do that." She sobered quickly. "I want to, I really do." She darted a quick look at him. "You've been more helpful than anything. Thank you."

"No problem."

No sense letting her know how reluctant he'd been.

"Things will look better when the power is back on and you hire some experienced cowboys or two."

She continued tracing a pattern, her eyes watching her finger.

"Right?" Cody asked. "I'll help you interview if that's what you're worried about."

Looking at him she shook her head.

"You know, Cody Fallon, you're really a nice man. You don't give up, do you? I'll have to see."

"About?"

"Calling on you when time to interview a cowboy."

"Okay, then. It's set. In the meantime, your phone is off and your power is off. I can call the power company from home to get an update on when it'll be fixed."

She shook her head.

"It's not necessary. I know when it'll be on."

"And that is?"

"Soon."

"Soon," he repeated. "That's your favorite word."

"It's the best I've got right now."

He decided to call the power company anyway and see if there was anything they could do to expedite repairs. A ranch needed power. The generator was good enough to limp along, but unless it was a big set up like the Rocking F had, it only was good for the short haul.

"Want to come over to the house to spend the night?" he asked, suddenly thinking about all the things not powered by an emergency generator.

He rose and went to the refrigerator and opened it. Dark and warm.

"There's nothing in there. I cleaned it out already."

"How long has the power been out?" he asked as he closed it.

"Since before I got here. There was really some gross stuff in there."

"Get your stuff. You're coming home with me."

"I beg your pardon?"

"We've got guest rooms galore and a hot shower with your name on it," he said wondering what she'd been doing the last several days without hot water.

"Tempting. I'd love a long hot shower," she said. "But I can't impose."

"No imposition. You can have your choice of guest room, with private bath. My grandfather lives in the house, for propriety's sake. And I don't."

He didn't know why he added that last part.

"Oh," she grinned. "Well, then, just one night. Thank you."

She rose. "I'll get a change of clothes and some stuff and be right back."

She snatched up a candle and disappeared into the rest of the house.

Cody went outside. He'd melt if he stayed in the house any longer. He walked over to the corral. Two of the horses came to the fence when he approached. Starlight nickered softly.

"Hey, old girl, how you holding up. Cushy place here, no work if the woman can't even get a saddle on you."

He scratched behind the horse's ears and patted her neck. He heard Holly shut the back door and then the screen.

She walked across the yard a swollen backpack on her shoulder.

He walked to the truck and opened the passenger door for her.

"I can drive," she said, hesitating.

"I'll take you and bring you back in the morning," he said.

She considered it another moment then nodded and climbed up into his truck.

In less than ten minutes Cody pulled into the yard of the Rocking F ranch. Wouldn't his family be surprised at what he brought home.

Seth and Jarred were sitting on the porch when Cody drove in. He stopped by the front of the house to let his guest off. Since this was her first visit, he knew his mother would want her to be treated like a special guest.

The two men rose and walked to the truck when Cody went around to open the passenger door.

"Ah, we have a guest," Seth said. "Welcome, my dear."

"Hi Mr. Fallon," she said, hopping down and pulling her backpack from the truck.

"It's Johnson, but call me Seth, please."

He looked at Cody.

"Power's still off at her place," Cody said as if that explained it all.

"Holly, this is my older brother Jarred."

"Nice to meet you," Holly murmured.

She was invited inside. Stepping inside the air conditioned house some moments later felt like heaven. She smiled at the men, a startled look when she saw Jarred in the light.

"Wow, you two look so much alike. You're not twins are you?"

Jarred shook his head. "Thankfully, no."

"Hey," Cody said in mock indignation.

"Ignore those two. Can I get you something to drink? Did you already have dinner?" Seth asked, stepping in between Cody and Holly.

"I'm fine, really."

"Told her she could take a hot shower. Let her pick her room," Cody said, standing near the door.

He watched his brother and Holly. She was pretty even with slightly red eyes. Sometimes he and Jarred liked the same woman. Not that he was liking Holly exactly. More like concerned for her. Felt responsible since he'd seen her first.

"I'll take you up," Jarred said.

He flicked a glance at Cody.

"See you at breakfast."

6

Holly looked at Cody and smiled. "Thank you," she said. Turning she followed Jarred up the stairs. Cody had said he didn't live in the large ranch house. She wondered where he did live.

"Your choice, this one's nice or you can have the one across the hall," Jarred said, stopping by an open door. The room was lovely. Done in tones of blue, it was spacious and beautifully furnished.

"This is perfect. Thank you."

"The bath is through the door on the right," he said, pointing to the door. "Let us know if you need anything."

"I'll be fine. And up early."

"We eat breakfast in the bunkhouse at six."

"Sounds perfect," she said with a straight face.

Six! Good heavenly days, she had better get to sleep soon if she didn't want to sleep late. She couldn't face Cody if she did. He'd been so kind. Nicer to her than her own mother.

"Good night, Jarred. It's nice to meet you."

"Good night."

He closed the door. Holly heard his boots on the hall and down the stairs before the sound faded.

She relished the coolness of the room. And the availability of hot water. She felt like a wimp breaking down in front of

Cody like she had. Things would look better in the morning. She went to the bathroom and immediately began the water for her shower.

Shampooing her head a short time later felt heavenly. And her spirits rose the longer she stayed in the shower.

Her friend Brittany had agreed to pick up her car and put it up for sale. Holly told her where the pink slip was and planned to fax a letter in the morning giving her formal permission to sell it. She could expect several thousand dollars for the car. Enough to get the power back on and the phone. Maybe hire a cowboy or two to buy some time to get some cattle sold.

That would be the first step. A crash course in animal husbandry would help, but she wasn't sure how to get that and still do what was needed around the ranch.

Slipping into bed a short time later, she turned out the light. She could hear gentle murmur of voices outside. The men had resumed their seats on the porch she guessed. Didn't they need to get to bed soon to get up with the sun? She hoped she'd wake up in time.

Despite being tired, Holly slept fitfully. She awoke shortly after five and decided to get up and ready for the day. With her luck if she finally fell back to sleep, it would be to sleep through breakfast. And the thought of a hot meal instead of granola bars had her throwing off the covers.

She was still a little stiff from riding the other day, but nothing like the day after. She needed to get back on a horse and build some stamina.

Maybe today when Cody took her home she could get him to saddle Starlight before he left. She could pull it off the mare, just not get it up on her back without whacking her silly.

She packed her things in the backpack and turned back to the bed. She pulled the coverlet up, wondering if she should strip it or leave it. Deciding to leave it, she left the room, her own new boots sounding on the wooden floor as she walked down the stairs.

They had said last night breakfast was in the bunkhouse. She didn't know where it was but figured she could find it.

She saw Cody's truck a short distance away and turned to walk to it to toss her backpack in.

It would be impossible to miss how pristine the ranch appeared. Such a contrast to her dad's place it made her heart ache. The house was huge, which she could have guessed last night by the empty guest rooms. Two stories, it gleamed white in the early sun, with deep green shutters and trim. There were flowers galore, in two neat beds by the front porch and in hanging containers by the porch pillars. The drive way was graveled, a bit hard to walk on, but a fine way to keep the dust down.

She looked at the large barn, deep red with white trim. It looked freshly painted. There were two large corrals on either side, with more horses in them than she could count.

Beyond that she saw a row of small houses. How cute they were, marching side by side away from the barn area.

To the left was a large building that had to be the bunkhouse.

Just then Cody came out of one of the small houses. He saw her right away and walked toward her. She met him part way.

"Good morning, sleep well?" he asked.

"Good morning. I did, thank you. I assume that's the

bunkhouse?" she said, gesturing toward the large wooden building.

"Yep."

"Do you eat all your meals there?"

"Mostly. When my folks are home, we eat what mom cooks if she's in the mood. But my folks believe our cowboys are as important to the ranch as anyone, so we usually eat together. Carlos is the cook and a good one to boot."

When Holly entered the bunkhouse she saw the large dining area to the left with a long trestle table and chairs on both sides. Several men were already seated with a plate in front of them. Two were filling cups at the coffee urn on the long counter against the far wall.

Conversation ceased immediately as everyone looked at Holly and Cody.

"This is Holly Braddock, from the Bar-B-Bar."

Cody then began introducing the men starting at one end of the table and going around to the other. "And Carlos," he said last when the cook came from the kitchen.

"I'll try to remember all the names," she said shyly, knowing she didn't have a chance.

Jarred and Seth came in just as she began eating the mound of scrambled eggs on her plate. Cody was right, Carlos was a great cook.

She watched and listened to the discussions as the men talked about what they'd be doing all day. Apparently from what was said, there was another brother, Kyle, who was out on the range. Where he'd spent the night. How large was the Rocking F that he couldn't get home at night? So far it sounded quite a bit larger than her father's property.

She felt defensive on behalf of the Bar-B-Bar. Could she possibly get it back in shape so it'd look as good as this ranch? She hoped so. Her wish was it would look as pristine as the Rocking F by the time her father came home.

Fat chance of that happening.

She'd be lucky to get the power back on by then.

How long did it take to sell a car?

"Holly?"

She looked at Cody.

"Sorry, I was thinking, did you say something?"

"Pedro asked if you're interested in talking to his cousin. He wants to move here and needs a job. He's a good hand—at least that's what Pedro says."

"And if he's not it would show poorly on me," one of the cowboys said with a sheepish grin. "He better be really good or I'll stomp him in the ground."

She assumed it was Pedro vouching for the cousin.

"Sure, when will he be in town?"

"In a couple of days," Pedro said. "I'll tell him to come see you."

She nodded, hoping her car would sell by then. She hated to interview anyone and have to say there was no power.

Come to think of it, she should check the bunk house. She hadn't even been inside this visit. She could at least get that ready for habitation in hopes she'd have money enough soon.

She glanced at Cody when she thought of soon. He was right, she used it a lot, hoping things would change.

He was silent during the meal. At least when she was paying attention. Was he not a morning person? She was. Though usually not up this early, she did her best work and thinking in the morning.

She wondered when Cody did his best work.

Someone said something about a pumper and the talk veered into mechanical jargon. Was it a well pump they talked about? Did her father have any wells? One of the things Cody had talked about was checking the watering places on the ranch.

She wished her father had a map of the property so she'd know where to start looking.

No one lingered over breakfast and Holly didn't want to be the last one done. She finished her coffee and refused a second cup. She'd love to linger over coffee, listen to the men talk, maybe even ask a question or two. But one by one they finished, carried their dishes to the kitchen and left–always with a word to her.

This would be her goal. Get her father's ranch functioning like this one. Maybe not on as large a scale, but where the hired help was as important as the owners–appreciated and respected.

"You ready?" Cody asked.

"Yes." She rose and gathered her plate, utensils and cup.

"I'll take them," Cody said, holding out his hand.

"I can manage," Holly said with a smile. "Thanks, though."

She was curious to see the kitchen. Stepping inside she immediately noticed the industrial size stove and huge refrigerator. Steam rose from the sink where Cody dumped his plate. She followed suit and smiled at Carlos.

"Thank you, that was delicious," she said.

"Pleasure, ma'am," he said, He looked at Cody. "Lunch packed, one for Miss Holly, too." He jerked his head toward the left.

Holly looked. There were still several lunch bags lined up on the counter.

"Thanks." Cody said. "Come on, grab one and we'll head out."

"I didn't expect lunch, too," she said as they walked back to Cody's truck.

Someone had hooked up a horse trailer behind it and she could hear a horse moving inside.

"I told Carlos we'd be riding out to look at the watering holes. We don't want to have to come back for lunch."

"Of course not."

That meant all day on the horse again. She hoped she was up to it.

Once the horses had been fed and watered, Cody leaned against the corral fence, then stepped away.

"This is about to fall over," he said.

Pushing and pulling the support pole, it moved and wobbled.

"Don't make it worse," she protested. "It's on the list."

"What list?"

"Of things to do around here."

Cody looked at her.

"A list," he repeated.

"So I'll know what to see to first. You know, find horses, check water holes, fix corral fence."

"You planning on doing this all yourself?"

She looked away, uncertainty in her expression.

"What I can," she said.

"Or hire some guys to get it done. And there aren't any more horses loose."

"How do you know?"

"I asked your dad when I saw him. He confirmed four is all he has right now. Guess Ed had his own horses. So it's fence riding and watering holes today."

She nodded.

"I'll run into the house and get my hat and put on some sun screen and be ready to ride," she said, taking off at a quick walk.

Cody unloaded Smoke from the back of the horse trailer and led him to the corral fence. He slung the lunches in a saddlebag on the back of the gelding. He called Starlight and put a halter on her. In no time he had her saddled and ready to go.

He wondered when Holly was going to come clean about what was going on around the ranch. He didn't have time for games. There was work to be done. This wasn't some on-again, off-again vacation for her. The ranch was in shambles and needed serious attention to get it going again.

She came out with a brand new cowboy hat on her head. Her arms were covered with a long sleeve shirt and the jeans looked a bit more broken in than when he'd first seen them. She still looked beautiful and too feminine to be riding the range.

"Ready," she said, coming up to Starlight. "Thanks for saddling the horse."

"You need to learn how," he said tightening the cinch.

"I know how, these saddles are really heavy and she's tall."

He nodded. "Maybe I could build you a platform so

you're closer to the height of the horse. That'll give you more leverage."

"That's a great idea."

"Another thing to add to your list," he said, mounting up and waiting for her.

He led the way out of the yard and stopped, looking around.

She came up beside him. "What?"

"Trying to decide where to start. On our joint fence, I'd say. If there're any problems I can get one of the men to fix it. Then we ride the perimeter until we complete the circuit."

"So we're checking the entire fence today?"

"And the watering holes. And maybe take a tally of cattle. And be on the look out for any situation that needs attention."

"Like?"

They urged the horses into a walk.

"Like a steer down with a broken leg. Or a carcass where a mountain lion's invaded. Or a dozen other things that need to be watched for."

Cody spurred his horse and broke into a canter. Cody relished the cool morning air against his face as Smoke ran into the open pasture land. The horse was raring to go. Small clumps of trees and shrubs dotted the gently rolling hills. From time to time he saw cattle grazing. Making a mental note of the number and rough location, he continued to the property line.

When they reached a barbed wire fence separating the Bar-B-Bar from the Rocking F, he slowed his mount to a walk. Holly followed suit, breathing hard.

"That was great!" she exclaimed, her face delighted with the ride.

He was struck again with how pretty she was. And how out of place she seemed in this setting.

"Now we walk. Did you notice the cattle we passed?"

"Yes. I counted twenty-five near that one group of trees and lots more than I could count when we crested that last rise."

"Lots more won't give you a good estimate of how many head you have."

Her face lost some exuberance.

"Do I need to go back and count?"

"No. I estimate a hundred. That'll be enough for now. When you need to know the exact amount, you can do a tally. Today's top priorities are different."

She nodded.

Cody had to give her some credit for counting the small bunch. He didn't know when he'd learned to estimate number of head based on what he saw. Counting each one would take more time than he wanted to spend today. An estimate was close enough.

He wondered how big Frank's herd was. Cody hadn't seen a cross fence. Didn't Frank rotate grazing land?"

"So tell me all I need to know," Holly said as they began riding along side the fence.

On the other side was the Rocking F ranch. A mile or more along the fence they'd come to the recently repaired gate that let the Bar-B-Bar cattle in.

"All you need to know for what?"

"To run this ranch until my dad's better," she said.

"Honey, that'll take you ten years or more. Not one day."

"I'm not your honey and don't be condescending. Tell me some of the basics. I'll pick up more as I get involved."

Cody's lips twitched. He wanted to laugh at her huffy tone. She kept trying, he'd give her that.

"Okay. You ask me something. I don't know where to start."

The rest of the morning Holly asked a question, he'd give her an answer, which would lead to more questions.

They were almost at the farthest reach of the ranch when noon arrived. Cody needed a tree and he expected she'd need to relieve herself as well. He spotted a thick copse of trees and sage, and headed for it. The shade would help while they ate, and there'd be enough privacy for them both.

"What's in the trees? We haven't gone to any of the other trees we've seen," she asked.

"Time to stop for lunch and take a bathroom break," he replied as they arrived in the scant shade beneath the tree's spreading limbs.

He dismounted and loosened the cinch on Smoke, letting the horse nibble at the sparse growth beneath the tree.

He looked up at Holly who was looking around the area.

"Bathroom break?" she said, looking down at him.

"I can use a tree. Thought you'd like a bit more privacy. Over yonder it's thick and I'll keep my back turned."

Her face scrunched up in contemplation. Then with a sigh, she nodded and slid off the horse, landing with a thump.

Cody thought she'd fall to the ground, but she clung to the saddle and got her legs under her. Still holding the reins, she began to stiffly walk toward him. Thrusting the reins into his hands, she continued walking until he could hear her rustle among the dead fall. Then silence.

Since they had stopped at a watering hole about a half hour ago, he knew the horses would be okay. He tethered Starlight and then waited, gazing off into the area they'd just patrolled. So far the fence was tight every where. They'd come to one cross fence, so Frank did rotate his herd. After the perimeter fencing, they'd have to check that one.

Holly came back.

"Thank you, your turn."

She came to stand by him, her back to the grove.

Once finished, Cody brought down the saddle bags and sat in the shade.

"Chow," he said.

She turned and went to join him. When he held out a hand wipe she looked startled as she reached out to accept it.

"Hey, we want to stay healthy. Do you know how dirty it gets ranching?"

"I guess I thought cowboys were too tough for that."

"Humph."

He held out the bag Carlos had prepared for her and dug into his own.

When the first pangs of hunger had subsided, he looked at her.

"I checked with the power company this morning. They don't show a power outage anywhere."

She looked at him, then looked away. Taking another bite of her sandwich, she gazed off into the distance.

"So what's the real story?" he persisted.

"Power was turned off," she said at last.

"When and why?"

"I don't know when, it's been off since I arrived. And why do you think Dad didn't pay the bill?"

Cody thought about that.

"How late is he?"

"Months. I went to have it turned on, but didn't have enough money with me. I have to wait until I get some to pay it off before they'll turn it back on. Until then I guess I'll use the generator as much as I can."

"How much?"

She hesitated a moment, then told him.

He whistled. "Whoa, that's a lot."

She nodded.

"So you're expecting some money? From your mom?"

She shook her head. "I'm having a friend sell my car. Once I get that money, it'll be able to do a lot."

She looked at him. "Like turn on the power, get the phone running and hire a cowboy or two to help out."

"Then what?"

"What do you mean?"

"Unless you have some really fancy car that'll bring in a ton of money, how long will that last, especially catching up the past due bills."

"Long enough to sell some cattle or something to bring in some money."

He studied her for a moment.

"What?"

"Nothing. Finish eating, we need to get going if we're going to finish today. Your dad has a bigger spread than I thought."

Holly finished her lunch, wishing she could kick off her boots and lay back in the shade and sleep the afternoon away. Her legs ached. Her back felt permanently out of whack and she was hot and grubby.

Glancing again at Cody, she was struck by how he looked perfectly at home in the heat and dust. He loved ranching, that was evident by the way he'd explained things to her. She could hear the enthusiasm in his tone, his satisfaction from knowing his livelihood inside and out.

She felt cheated. Her father should have included her in the ranch more when she was growing up. Not insisted she spend her teenage summers at resorts or in Europe but have her come to learn what she could about her heritage.

Acknowledging she could have done more, too, she still felt the responsibility had rested with him. He was the parent. He'd been the adult for most of her life. It was only now when she was really needed did he let her help.

And she was little help. What would she have done if Cody Fallon had not driven the ranch horses back when she'd been home?

Cody balled his trash in his bag and rose.

Holly quickly followed suit. No matter what, she didn't want to be more of a burden on this cowboy than she could help.

"Ready to ride?" he asked.

She plastered a smile on her face and tried to muster some enthusiasm.

"Let's go!"

Getting on the horse was a monumental task. She promised herself she'd find a way to take a long hot bath tonight no matter what. She owed her body some relief.

The heat continued to build and they stopped at another watering trough which was full of water, even spilling over by the lazy pumping action of the windmill. The horses drank long and deep. She fantasized about falling face first into the cool water and letting the rest of the day take care of itself.

Cody didn't even dismount. So neither did she.

As they continued, she remembered his saying her father's horses needed to build up stamina before they could be used again. Looked like she did, too. She was so tired she could hardly stay upright. While Cody looked as energetic as he had this morning. So much for Pilates classes.

"Will we be back in time for me to visit my dad?" she asked as the afternoon waned.

"Don't see why not. After supper, most likely."

She'd toyed with the idea of skipping supper and falling into bed as soon as she got off the horse.

"We'll drive in together if you like."

When they reached the house, Holly felt as if she'd had a cram course in ranching. She knew she wouldn't remember all Cody had explained, but she had a better understanding and knew who to go to when she had more questions.

To her immense relief, Cody offered to unsaddle Starlight and feed the horses. She could have kissed him. He didn't even make it seem like he thought she couldn't manage.

Which he had to once she got off the horse. Her legs gave way and she plopped down in the dust.

"You okay?" he asked, reaching down a hand to pull her up.

"I will be," she said through gritted teeth.

Her legs felt numb. Was that worse than burning with use?

She wasn't sure, but tried to casually walk to the corral fence. She didn't care how loose it was, it could hold her up until she could walk halfway decently.

She watched as Cody efficiently worked, turning both his horse and Starlight into the corral. He fed all the horses, went to start the generator to be able to fill the water trough. Holly knew she should be doing that, but she simply could not do it tonight.

Tears welled. She blinked them away furiously. She refused to appear as a weepy female around this strong cowboy. She'd cried enough yesterday. From now on, she was one tough western woman.

If she could only walk.

"Ready?" he asked, coming out of the shed that housed the pump and generator some time later.

"For?"

"To get back to the ranch house, clean up and eat so we can see your dad," he said patiently as if explaining to a child.

She toyed with the idea of staying home, of doing for herself. But the thought of a bath was too tantalizing.

"Thank you. As soon as I can get the power on, I'll be able to manage."

"Your refrain–soon – I can manage," he teased. "Come on, neighbors are always welcomed at the Rocking F."

To her embarrassment, Holly fell asleep on the short drive to the Rocking F. Cody shook her gently when they arrived and she blinked being woken.

"Oh, sorry," she said.

"No problem. Dinner's in a half hour. In the bunk house again. See you there," he said, getting out of the truck and heading for the barn.

She hopped out and walked to the front door, her legs feeling like jelly. Her quickly packed backpack had another change of clothes and a fresh nightie. She wished she could bathe and hop into bed. Instead, she'd take a quick shower, dress and get to dinner so they could go see her father.

Dare she tell him all she was doing? He had to be aware of what needed doing. Would it comfort him to know she was taking over? Or would he worry even more?

7

Dinner proved to be a great distraction to the constant worry about the ranch. Holly felt more comfortable around the men now and was even beginning to associate names with faces. She laughed at some of the stories which she knew had to be exaggerated to entertain her.

When asked about her day, she tried to make the routine ride sound as exciting as she could.

Cody watched her but didn't add anything. Twice she smiled slyly at him challenging him to curb the exaggerations. But he merely smiled and look at his food.

When dinner was finished, Cody drove into town.

"I'll give you some time with your dad alone if you like," he said when they reached the convalescent hospital.

"No, I'll keep the visit short. He'll want to see you, too, I'm sure."

Frank Braddock was propped up in the hospital bed watching TV when they entered. He slowly turned his head and smiled when he saw Holly. The smile was lopsided as one half of his face didn't respond.

Holly rushed over to give him a hug.

She wanted him to get better faster than he seemed to be.

"Hi Daddy," she said with a smile. "I brought Cody to visit, too. Rather, he brought me."

Cody stepped inside, holding his hat in his hands.

"Evening, Frank. Good to see you. Do you need anything?"

Frank slowly shook his head.

Holly perched on the edge of his bed while Cody took the chair nearby. She plunged into telling her father what they'd done today. How much she'd learned from Cody and how the cattle looked.

Frank seemed content to lie back and watch her talk. Once or twice he smiled.

When his eyes began to droop, Holly knew it was time to go.

"I may not be back tomorrow, but for sure the next day," she said.

If she was as tired tomorrow as today she didn't want him to expect her if she gave in and went to bed early. She loved her father, wanted to spend time with him, but she was so tired she was almost seeing crossed eyed.

"Did you think he looked better?" she asked Cody when they walked down the hall toward the front entrance.

"Honestly?"

She nodded, "Of course. Which I guess means you don't."

"I think he looks wiped out. I don't think he's going to recover as fast as we'd all like."

She sighed. "I know. I wanted to believe he looked better, but I don't think so. On the other hand, I didn't think he looked worse."

Cody stopped by the front desk and asked the nurse if the doctor happened to be around.

He had left for the day, she said.

Holly looked at him.

"Did you want to talk to Dr. Burns?"

"I wanted you to. To find out more what's going to be needed and a time frame."

"It'll probably be a couple of months before Mr. Braddock will be well enough to leave," the nurse said. "He could surprise us and recover faster, but I wouldn't count on it," she said sympathetically. "If you're looking for a time frame. Of course, I'm not the doctor."

"That gives us a time frame. Do you know if he's expected to make a full recovery?" Cody said.

"Hard to say. He could of course."

Holly understood. He could, but it was unlikely.

"So what's a rancher to do if he can't run his ranch?" Holly asked a moment later when they got into the truck.

"Hire people he can trust," Cody responded.

She gazed out the window as they sped back to the Rocking F. She had never tried to pin the doctor down on her dad's prognosis, content to hear he should make a complete recovery. But should make and doing it could be two different things.

What if he didn't ever walk again?

Or worse, never talked again?

She could run things if she knew more. And had some help.

At least she thought she could. Was she fooling herself?

What choice did she have? Where would her dad go if he couldn't live on the Bar-B-Bar? What would he do the rest of his life?

"It's a mess, isn't it?" she said.

"Life often is," Cody responded.

When they reached home, Jarred and Seth were sitting on the porch a big pitcher of iced tea on the table between them.

"I'm going up to bed, if you gentlemen won't think I'm rude," Holly said when she climbed the stairs.

"I expect you're tried," Seth said. "Run along and don't worry about us. How's your dad?"

"Hanging in there, I guess. No real improvement. Good night."

She headed for the guest room she'd used before. In no time she slipped into her nightie and crawled between the covers wondering if she'd be able to get out of bed in the morning. Pulling the covers over her head and waiting until everything got better sounded like a much better plan.

She was almost asleep, lulled by the soft murmur of voices from the porch when she hears a sharper tone. She couldn't hear the words, but it sounded as if the Fallon men were in disagreement about something.

Nothing to do with her, she hoped. In seconds she was asleep.

Holly came down stairs the next morning to an empty house. Checking her watch she saw she had slept in a bit late and everyone was probably already eating breakfast, if not already finished. She hesitated about going to the bunk house and having everyone make fun of her for sleeping in, but the food Carlos made was too delicious and nourishing to pass up. She didn't know when she'd have another hot meal unless she drove into town.

Entering the large dining hall she was grateful to Seth when the older man spotted her and pointed to an empty place beside him.

"Good morning. Get your breakfast and come sit here by an old man."

She murmured a good morning to all and hurried to the sideboard where there was still plenty of food. Heaping eggs and grits on her plate, she took a muffin and before she could get her coffee, one of the ranch hands had filled a mug for her and handed it to her.

"Thank you," she said with a bright smile.

She thought it was Pedro but was too uncertain to say the name.

She sat at the table and looked around. Most of the men were still eating, though two were nursing coffee, empty plates in front of them.

Cody looked up and nodded.

"Sorry I slept in so late," she said.

Six in the morning wasn't so late, but for these working men it probably was.

"No problem," he said.

She ate while conversation resumed and the men discussed the different tasks Jarred was assigning. When he told Cody he needed to get to town and get some more baling wire, his brother didn't protest.

She hid a smile. From the limited interaction she'd seen between the brothers, it was a miracle Cody didn't protest. He and Jarred seemed rarely to agree.

Looking back and forth between the two of them, she wondered if she sensed some tension.

Probably her imagination.

"I'll be taking you home after breakfast," Seth said genially. "I can help feed those critters in your corral, too, before coming back here."

"Thank you. I hate to be a bother."

She refused to look at Cody. Why wasn't he taking her back? Trying to squash the disappointment that flooded, she concentrated on finishing breakfast so she wouldn't hold Seth up. She knew from what Jarred said there were things needing Seth's attention on the ranch.

Once on the road, she wondered if she could ask about Cody, why he wasn't taking her home on the way to town. Not that it was on the way, but he'd already be out and about.

Probably tired of babysitting someone who knew so little about ranching.

"Need to get your mail?" Seth asked as they approached the turn to the Bar-B-Bar.

"Yes."

She realized she hadn't picked up the mail in a couple of days. She hopped out of the truck at the mailbox, not surprised to find the box almost full. Mostly magazines, fliers, junk mail and a few bills.

"Thanks. I need to remember to check it every day," she said getting back into the truck.

She and Seth made short work of feeding the horses. He started the generator for her and they made sure the water tank was full.

"You'll need more gas for the generator, it's about out," he said as the machine droned on in the background.

"I'll get some the next time I'm in town," she said. "Thanks for all your help, Seth. I don't want to hold you up."

"Not a problem. That's what neighbors are for–helping out when someone needs it. Tell your father I'll be in later this week to visit."

She watched the truck as it left, thinking of his comment. She'd begun to think Cody's help was more than just a neighbor helping a neighbor.

"Silly, as if he'd have any interest in me. I can't even saddle a horse. How would a cowboy find that appealing?"

Going inside, she sorted the mail, tossing the junk stuff in the trash and opening the two bills. One was from the feed store with a large red past due stamp across the front. As if she didn't already know that.

The other was from the ER department of the hospital where her dad had be taken when discovered after his stroke. She blinked at the cost. At the bottom was a notation no insurance company on record, could he please provide information on medical insurance coverage.

"Do you have medical insurance, daddy," she said softly.

Her heart sank. What if he hadn't made the premium payments? A serious illness like this could bankrupt a wealthy person, much less someone already teetering on the brink.

She felt overwhelmed again.

How soon could Brit sell her car? Maybe she should lower the price for a quick sale. Though Holly needed as much money as she could get out of it, it was her only source of cash for the time being.

The generator sputtered and went silent.

She listened to the silence for a long moment, then rose to take care of priorities. She needed that well running for the horses.

Heading into town, with three gas cans in the back of the pickup, she tried to remain optimistic. She'd visit her dad first, then get the gas, and a few things to eat. She couldn't keep sponging off the Fallons.

Especially now that she knew it didn't mean anything to Cody Fallon. Not that she went there just to see him.

Wryly she admitted that had played a big part. She'd wanted to see where he lived, how he lived, learn more about him. She was intrigued by the man. He was so different from men she knew at home. More rugged, more self confident, and competent. She couldn't imagine any of the men she'd dated in the past being able to mend a fence, rope a horse or know how to start a generator.

Her father looked better that morning. He seemed more alert and animated, though his speech was still impossible to understand. And he struggled so hard with it, it was painful to see.

"Oh, Seth said he'd be in to see you later," she said.

Frank nodded, his face giving his lopsided smile. "Gggoood mmm—"

"Man?" she said, her heart aching as he tried so hard. "They're all good out there."

She told him about caring for the horses, about her visit to the Rocking F. Then asked about insurance.

"I can't find anything in the office about insurance. You have it, right?"

Frank nodded.

"Where would the policies be?"

He tried to say something, but she couldn't understand him at all.

"It's okay, Dad, I'll find the paperwork."

She felt relieved he had insurance. Once she could tell the hospital it would be one less thing to worry about.

She stayed until her dad grew tired, then left.

She checked her phone, dead. Not having service at the ranch, she forgot all about it. Where could she get a charge? Did the local coffee shop offer charging? She'd check it out. She wanted to get it charged while in town. Not that she'd need it on the ranch, but in case she had any messages.

Entering Rosie's Café a short time later, she didn't see anything like Starbucks with charging stations and work space. This was an old fashioned coffee shop. Taking a seat at the counter, she laid her phone down.

"What can I get you," the young waitress behind the counter came over and smiled at her. She had auburn hair, bright blue eyes and looked to be about Holly's age.

"Coffee would be great. Know where I can get a charge for my phone?"

"Got the cord?" the waitress asked as she brought a mug and the coffee carafe.

"Yes."

Holly brought it out of the purse. After the coffee was poured, the waitress took phone and cord and disappeared into the kitchen. She came right back.

"Stay as long as you like for the coffee and when you're ready to leave, I'll get it for you."

"Thanks."

"I'm Carrie Sue," the waitress said. "I know most folks who live around here. You visiting?"

"For a while. I'm Holly Braddock, Frank Braddock's daughter."

"Oh, I didn't know he had any kids. How's he doing? We all heard about his stroke."

"Doctor says he'll get better, but it's going lots slower than I'd like."

"I bet. Tell him hey for me when you see him."

"I just came from there. His speech is so difficult to understand and the frustration is really evident when he tries to talk."

"Haven't seen a lot of him lately," Carrie Sue said, spotting a customer across the room needing her. "Let me know if I can do anything for him," she said as she headed for the other customer.

Holly sipped her coffee and made plans. Once she got the money from selling her car, she'd see about more feed for the horses.

The Fallon men were generous in the portions for the ones they were trying to fatten up, so she was going through the feed faster than she expected. She had some more money left on her credit card. After that, some things to eat for herself, then the gas and back to the ranch.

She thought she'd have time today to figure out how to saddle Starlight and ride out to see if she could find any of water holes on her own. She wished again there was a map of the ranch.

When she went to the feed store, she'd ask the proprietor about selling cattle. He could probably tell her the best contacts.

Or she could ask Cody. He'd know.

She wondered if he and his family ran the same kind of cattle her father did. When was the best time to sell? Could she hold off to get a better price?

She'd begun to comb through her father's records to reconcile how much he owed and if there were any assets—beyond the cattle—she could liquidate. She'd try to finish up when she returned home. Better to do that in daylight when she had light.

First thing she was going to do when she got her money was to get that electricity turned on. She didn't know how women in the olden days managed without.

"Want some more?" Carrie Sue asked, the coffee about ready to pour.

"One more cup," Holly said. "What's with all the colorful postcards on that wall?" she asked, looking at the wall to the left. It was covered with post cards from all over the world.

Carrie Sue smiled. "My boyfriend sends them. He's a reporter, gets assignments all over and always sends me a card."

"Wow, that's quite a collection. How cool."

"One day I'd like to visit some of those places. But for now, this is home," Carrie Sue said cheerfully.

Holly rose and carried her cup over to see them closer. Istanbul, Cairo, Paris, London, Cape Town. This guy did get around.

"Carrie Sue," a familiar voice sounded behind her. Holly turned to see Cody Fallon taking the seat next to where she'd been sitting.

"Hey, Cody, what're you up to?"

"Had some business in town. I'd like a cup of Joe and a piece of Harry's apple pie."

"Coming right up. Want that heated with ice cream?"

"Yep." He smiled at her.

Holly studied him for a moment before he realized she was there. He looked surprised to see her, then smiled at her.

She caught her breath as her heart rate kicked up a notch.

"Hey, Holly. How's your dad?"

"Doing about the same."

She returned to the seat and turned slightly to better face him.

"I'd like an in depth briefing from the doctor, but he wasn't there this morning. I asked his nurse to schedule an appointment. Like you, I'm ready for a time frame on his recovery."

"Makes a difference in making plans. What will you do if he takes longer than you can stay?" he asked.

"I'm staying until he doesn't need me any more," Holly said firmly.

Carrie Sue placed a large slice of pie, steaming hot with ice cream starting to melt on top, in front of Cody. She filled a mug for him and topped off Holly's again.

Casting a watching gaze around the room, she leaned against the counter joining the conversation.

"My aunt Eloise had a stroke. She still uses a walker. Lives in a home. Of course she's seventy-nine, not as young as Frank. He's what, in his fifties?"

Holly nodded.

"That's something else you should find out," Cody said. "Is his recovery going to be complete or will there be limitations. Restrictions that would impact his ability to run his ranch."

"That's my one fear. But if I get some good cowboys, I can do my best until he's better."

Cody dug into the pie.

"Maybe, but you don't know much."

Holly sighed. "I know. If daddy's speech would improve

I could run everything by him."

"Knowing where you stand will make a difference," Carrie Sue said.

"That and learning more about how to run a ranch," Holly said with a wry smile. "Thanks for the coffee."

It was time to go. She had lots to do.

"I'll get your phone."

"Phone?" Cody asked.

"I forgot to charge it. Not being able to use it on the ranch, I forget about it."

"You could have charged it at our place."

"I just said I forget about it. That would have been too easy, I guess."

Carrie Sue returned with the phone and cord.

When Holly opened her purse and took out her wallet, Cody shook his head.

"I've got this."

She protested. "I don't expect you to pay for my coffee."

"It's nothing. Go."

"Thank you. Carrie Sue, it was nice to meet you. I'll come back and check out more of those postcards."

Cody glanced over at the wall.

"When's he coming back to make an honest woman of you?"

Carrie Sue shrugged. "I haven't a clue. He's following the latest middle east skirmish. I just hope he's safe."

"Bye," Holly said as she left.

She checked her phone and was startled to find she had half dozen messages–all from Brit. Once in the truck, she played the messages.

"Holly, call me. Your mother won't give me the pink slip to sell the car."

"Holly, where are you? Call me about your car and your mother."

"Holly, this is Brit. Nothing is moving on the car sale."

Three more were along the same line. There were no messages from her mother, but Holly called her first.

"Hello, Holly," her mother answered on the second ring.

"Mom, Brit says you won't give her the pink slip. She needs that to sell my car."

"I'm not aiding and abetting you in throwing good money after bad. If your father can't manage his own affairs, you shouldn't be expected to do so. You need to turn it over to his attorney or someone and come home."

"Mom, I told you, I'm not coming home until Dad's back on his feet. I need that money."

"The ranch has managed for years without any money from you, I'm sure it'll manage for years to come."

Holly was reluctant to tell her mother anything about her father's financial situation. It was her car. If she wanted to sell it, that had nothing to do with her mother. And so she told her.

"Until you come to your senses or come home to get it yourself, it stays right where it is."

"And that is?"

"I put it in my safe deposit box right after Brittany tried to get it. Holly, I know this is making you angry, but I am doing what I think is right. Come home and we can discuss it. And, if once away from the influence of your father you still feel the same, well I can't stop you from selling the car. But you have to do it, not delegate it to Brittany."

"Mom, the air fare home is money I could use here. I need that money from the car."

Panic touched her. What if she couldn't get an influx of cash soon. How would she manage? She couldn't live off the neighbors for weeks on end. A couple of nights was one thing, but establishing residency there was definitely out of the question.

"If you want that pink slip, come home and get it."

With that the line was disconnected.

Holly wanted to throw her phone across the car, she was so angry. She gripped it tightly, wishing it was her mother. She was so angry. How dare her mother not give Brit the pink slip. The car was Holly's and had been from the time she graduated high school.

She tried to calm down before calling Brittany.

"Holly, your mom is a piece of work," Brit said when she answered.

"I know. I spoke to her and she won't give you the pink slip. She wants me to come home. She and my father haven't spoken in years, but you'd think she'd be a bit more compassionate about the situation. He can't manage on his own."

"How's he doing?"

"About the same as far as I can tell."

She'd been here almost a week and hadn't seen a single thing that looked better with her father. What if he never recovered? Then what?

"I've got some money I can lend you. How's that?"

"You're great, Brit. And I appreciate it. But there are other ways. Sorry for having to deal with my mother."

"What are you going to do?

"It's a cattle ranch, I'll sell some cattle. It's just it'll probably take a little while and I wanted some working capital right away. But I'll manage. How're thing going there?"

Brit filled her in on news of their friends. Holly was impatient to end the call, but stayed on for the sake of their friendship. The worry over the ranch almost swamped her. She tried to care about what Brit was sharing, but it seemed so frivolous compared to what she was dealing with.

Finally Brit wound down.

"I'll call again soon. Thanks again for trying to help," Holly said.

She slipped her phone into her purse and leaned her head against the headrest. She didn't have a clue how to manage from now on. Her one hope had been cash from her car. She didn't have any jewelry. She couldn't return her trip to Europe and get a refund.

Why had her father paid for that extravagance if he couldn't afford it?

"To show mom," she murmured. She'd bet her last dollar on that.

Cody left the café and turned toward her truck. She watched him a moment and saw when he realized she was still there. Altering his direction slightly, he came around to the driver's window.

"Trouble with the truck?"

She shook her head.

"Why are you still here then?"

"I had a couple of calls to make. I'm heading to the feed store now."

She hesitated a moment, then looked at him.

"I need to sell some cattle. How can I get the best price?"

"This isn't the best time to sell," he said slowly.

"That's as may be, but I need to get some cash fast."

He studied her for a moment.

"Thought you had some coming in soon."

"I thought so too, but found out I don't."

She was so angry with her mother. She wouldn't fly back to California to get the money if there was any other way.

"I can put you in touch with some buyers from Cheyenne. But this isn't a good time. You won't get top dollar."

"How does it work?"

Cody looked down the street thinking. Holly waited for him to answer.

He looked at her again.

"Come back inside. We need to sit down for this talk."

He held the door open for her and suggested they sit at a table in the back.

Carrie Sue was surprised to see them.

"What are you doing back so soon?" she asked.

"Something's come up. Could we have a menu? Might as well have lunch," Cody said as they walked to the empty table in the back.

Holly sat and looked at him. "All this to tell me how to contact someone in Cheyenne?"

"Nope."

He smiled at Carrie Sue when she brought the menu.

"Holler when you're ready," she said.

Holly decided quickly on a hot turkey sandwich. She was conscious she couldn't count on her next hot meal with the power out at the house. And she wasn't going to stay at her neighbors any more.

When their orders had been given, Holly looked at Cody. "Now what?"

"How about letting me lend you the money you need?"

8

Holly stared at him.

"What? Are you serious? You don't even know me. I tried the bank, I have no collateral, no job except trying to keep my dad's ranch going. I don't get it."

"Hey, people help people all the time," he said, feeling awkward. He thought she'd jump at the solution.

"Maybe some people, but I don't think that's a good idea. You could lose any money you lend me. I know next to zilch about running a ranch. What would you get out of it?"

"The knowledge I helped you."

She stared at him in disbelief.

"Like that's enough to spend money on. I truly think I can learn enough to be of help to my dad until he can take over, but not at the risk of any money you'd lose if you backed me."

He looked beyond her a minute, obviously in thought.

"How about this, I coach you, so I can make sure you know what you're doing. When it's time to sell at optimum prices, you can pay me back."

She shook her head.

"I don't know. We could end up having to sell the ranch to cover the money if selling cattle isn't enough."

Cody leaned back in his chair when Carrie Sue brought their plates.

"Call me if you need anything else," she said.

With a quick smile at each of them, she hurried back to the counter where two cowboys had come in and sat.

Holly didn't know if she could eat. Her stomach was churning, her mind spinning. Taking the money would be wrong, but oh how it could help. If she could get some help on the ranch it would go a long way to turning things around.

But she dare not take Cody's money. He could be just throwing it away if they couldn't repay him. Though she would repay it, if it took all her life.

What kind of return on investment would that be for him?

He began eating and she wished she had her normal appetite. Taking a bite, she was conscious of how good the turkey was. Taking another, she realized how hungry she was. It was some time before he spoke again.

"How about this, a partnership."

"What kind of partnership?" she asked.

"I'll buy into the ranch. We'll run it until it gets back in the black and then you can buy me out."

"Sell you part of my father's ranch?"

"Not sell part, think of me as a silent partner."

She looked at him suspiciously. "How silent?"

He grinned and she caught her breath. He looked sexy as anything and she couldn't focus on what he was saying.

"What? Say again," she prompted.

"Maybe not too silent. I could show you how to manage a ranch. Hire some cowboys, get the place back in shape and work with the herd to get the best price at market—when it's time."

"What if the bills overwhelm the ranch? Where would you be then?"

"If it comes to that, I'd take my share out of the sale of the ranch. But it won't come to that. I know something about cattle. Your dad has had a good spread over the years. It's only in the last bit of time or so that things turned dicey."

Like when he funded her extravagant trip through Europe, she thought. She could kick herself for not being more aware of the cost and how much it would strap the ranch.

"I don't know."

She couldn't make a quick decision. Yet, who would she talk it over with ? Her mother had made it crystal clear Holly should cut her loses and come home. Her father was still too fragile to require decisions. He needed rest and no stress.

Her best friend Brittany. She needed to talk it over with her. Granted she had no more ranching experience than Holly, but she had a good head on her and was impartial. She could tell Holly if her intense desire to run the ranch was merely guilt or if there was a chance to make it work.

"I'll think about it," she said.

He nodded. "Fine by me. Need anything while you're in town?"

"No, I'm good."

As good as she was going to get with her credit card limit. She wished she could pull this off herself, but she knew she couldn't.

"So why are you in town?" she asked, trying to show some semblance of normalcy.

"Need to do a few things for the ranch. Jarred acts like boss of the place, but it's mine as much as his. Still, I didn't mind coming in."

"When is a good time to sell cattle?" she asked.

"Depends on lots of things. One of them is how much they weigh. You need to do a tally of the calves and see how much they weigh, estimated of course. Then factor in the cost of growing them or selling for whatever you can get now."

"Tally, you said that before. How many head are we talking about?"

"I have no idea," Cody said. "I can ask my grandpa if he knows how many your father had. Or ask him."

"Do you think that would worry him? I don't want him stressed," she said.

"My guess is he's worried sick right now about what's going on out there. You can't hide the situation from him—he's a cattleman. He knows how much work is needed."

She hadn't thought about that.

"So maybe knowing you were helping me would go a long way in making him less stressed?"

"Could be." Cody finished his lunch. "You going to finish that?"

"Yes. Sorry, I'm trying to decide what to do. I need to talk to someone. Can I call you later and let you know?"

"Sure. Who's your friend?"

"Brittany Douglas. We've been friends since I was a little girl. She used to long to come with me in the summers to visit my dad, but we never were able to pull it off."

"Tell me about visiting your dad as a kid. I don't remember you. Your dad and mine have been friends for a long time."

"I sort of remember you. Or maybe it was one of your brothers. Anyway, when I visited it was only for a few weeks and my dad seemed to drop everything else to spend the days with me. I loved riding out to see the cows, play in the yard, ride in the truck. My mother never had a good word to say about the ranch, but I thought it was magical."

"How did your folks hook up if you mother didn't like ranching?"

"I don't know."

She realized she'd never asked.

"Isn't that weird. I never asked either of them. They divorced when I was really small. I just accepted things as they were."

She remembered her mother's scathing remarks, her frustration that Holly loved visiting her father and being on the ranch. It was dirty, smelly and isolated–all the things her mother hated.

"Not that it matters. They weren't married long," she said.

"Did she remarry?"

Holly shook her head.

"Frank didn't either."

She looked at him. "Is that significant?"

He shrugged. "Who knows? Interesting, however. Maybe they couldn't live together but didn't want anyone else."

"Or the marriage was so awful, both decided not to risk it again," she countered. She pushed her plate away. "I'm finished. I won't hold you up any longer. Thank you for lunch."

"Call me either way," he said as they stood.

She nodded and left while he was still paying.

Holly drove to a church and pulled into the empty parking lot. She had to call Brittany while she was still in town and had cell service. She hoped her friend could talk.

It was still morning in California. She'd be at work. Could she take a break?

The phone went to voice mail and Holly left a message to call her.

Since she had to stay in town to get the return call, she decided to go to the library to stock up on books about cattle ranching.

When it was noon in California, Holly went back to the truck in anticipation of her friend calling. She began reading as she waited.

Finally she gave up. She didn't know where Brit was or how soon she could call but Holly couldn't stay all day in the truck.

She swung by the hospital before heading home. Her father had just returned to his room from physical therapy and she was glad he was still awake.

"I won't stay, I know you'll want a nap. I wanted to tell you that you don't need to worry about the ranch. I have help. Cody Fallon's going to help out. He knows much more than I do, so he'll be right on top of things. Between us we can manage. So no worrying."

Her father tried to say something and Holly struggled to understand, but simply couldn't.

"I don't know what you're saying, Daddy, but please don't worry. We'll manage fine. I'm not going anywhere until you're completely better."

Cody watched Holly drive away and turned to walk to the bank. He'd had this out with his grandfather and Jarred last night. Neither one thought he knew what he was doing. But they didn't understand he just couldn't stand by and watch Holly struggle when she hadn't a clue what to do to run a cattle ranch. And he felt his father would want someone to help Frank. They'd been good friends for years.

He needed to transfer money, and liquidate some assets, to have the money they'd need on the Bar-B-Bar. He was seriously wanting to help. If not as a loan, then as part owner of the ranch. He made his family see reason with that suggestion, but wouldn't push the issue. It was a way to guard his investment, but he was less concerned about that than in getting the ranch operational again.

Robert Taylor, the bank president, greeted him and invited him into his office.

"What can I do for you today, Cody?" he asked after pleasantries were exchanged.

He explained his need for liquidity. With few questions, Robert nodded and quickly set in motion the necessary steps to transfer funds into Cody's checking account.

"Big step buying into a ranch," he said.

"It's not a done deal yet," Cody said. "But I've thought it through."

"The Bar-B-Bar's not doing well. You should get a big chunk for a good price," Robert said. "Frank took out a loan, not too big, but it's in arrears. And the ranch was security."

"We'll see," Cody said.

He suspected the banker would hold out for the lowest price he could get. Cody wanted to be fair. He needed to protect any investment, but he wasn't out to short change Holly or her father. And he wasn't sure she'd go for either a loan or the partnership.

Though it sounded to him like she was flat out of other options.

He finished at the bank and headed for the feed store to check out available help. If he did end up part owner of another ranch, he knew he'd be stretched pretty thin between his chores on the Rocking F and trying to give the new commitment his best.

Pedro's cousin had found another job in Colorado, so wouldn't be coming. So it was up to Cody to get some help.

There were a couple of help wanted posts on the bulletin board. One had been up for three months.

"No one interested in these jobs?" Cody asked Joe, the owner, who was stacking twenty pound dog food sacks.

"One is for Brian Orphry. No one wants to work for that crotchety old man. The other is looking for someone who can do cowboy work and also do shoeing. Not too many cowboys do both. Rocking F hiring?"

"No, not me. Bar-B-Bar may be soon." Cody said.

"Hmm, not likely anyone will respond to that one either. Ed did a thorough job of telling everyone and his brother how he got stiffed his last two months of pay."

"I heard," Cody responded.

If Holly accepted his offer, he'd settle up with Ed first thing. Get him to change his tune before he scared away every cowboy in thirty miles.

If Holly accepted.

Why did it matter to him if she did or didn't? He offered to help. If she said no, that was the end of it.

But he knew it wouldn't be the end. He didn't want to see the struggles she'd have to go through. Didn't want her living hand to mouth with a generator running a few hours a day. Didn't want her to watch the place fall apart and feel responsible until her father recovered.

He didn't know if Frank would ever be back to fighting form.

What would that do to Holly if he didn't fully recovered?

He never wanted to know.

Cody sat on the porch with his grandfather and Jarred after dinner that night. The discussion was centered on the possibility of hearing from his folks in the next day or two.

"It's been a month tomorrow, so I expect to hear from them in the morning," Seth said.

"Give or take a day," Jarred said rocking his chair back on two legs.

"So we hang around in the morning for a while. Won't hurt," Cody said.

Because of the time difference, the calls usually came in before nine in the morning.

"You settle anything with the Braddocks?" Jarred asked.

He'd been strongly opposed to Cody's involvement in the Bar-B-Bar when they discussed it last night.

Cody looked over to him.

"I made the offer. Now I'm waiting on the answer."

"I'm surprised she didn't accept on the spot," Jarred said.

"I was, too, come to that. As I see it, she's out of options if she hopes to keep the ranch going."

"Wonder if Frank wants to keep it going," Seth said.

"Why wouldn't he, it's been his life. His father and grandfather owned that ranch before him," Cody said.

He couldn't imagine a rancher not wanting to continue the work as long as he was able.

Ah, but would Frank be able?

"There is that. But look at the dynamics. He has no sons. His daughter isn't a rancher. He'd be better off selling it and finding a nice condo and doing something else. Just saying. It'll depend on his recovery," Seth said.

"Holly could run it, given enough time to learn," Cody said.

Jarred laughed sarcastically.

"Yeah, right. The pampered girl was a year in Europe, spending money like it was water. She stopped visiting her dad years ago. Ranching's not in her blood. She'd give it up even sooner than her mother did," Jarred said.

"Cynic. You don't know that," Cody said.

"Face it bro, she's pretty and has you interested. But if she wanted to be a rancher, you can bet she'd have been here every summer instead of ending visits when she was thirteen. She would have spent time here instead of a year in Europe after college. I've heard Frank and Dad talking. He's missed her every moment, but she rarely called, stopped her visits. Now suddenly she shows up guilty over her father's stroke and wants to be a savior for the ranch? I'm not buying it."

"You didn't see her. She's trying. She rode out with me twice, asking a dozen questions. Tried to sell her car to raise cash. I'm not sure she understands everything fully, but at least she's trying."

"Or giving the appearance of damsel in distress so the brave cowboy hero rides to her rescue," Jarred jeered.

"Jarred, you don't know that," Seth said.

Cody remained silent. Jarred had a point. She hadn't been involved at all with the ranch in a decade. She could think she could save the ranch but the first setback could send her hightailing it for California.

So maybe he should rescind the loan offer and stick with buying into the ranch. He knew he'd always have a part of the Rocking F. But with four brothers to share in the ranch, it wasn't the same as his own place. Not that a partnership with Frank assured him his own place.

How would he like being tied to Holly forever through joint ownership of the ranch?

It wouldn't come to that.

If she couldn't make it, she'd be glad to sell her portion.

On the other hand, if Frank recovered and bought him out, he'd recoup the money invested.

"Maybe I don't know that for sure," Jarred said. "But face facts. The woman knows nothing, is in an emotional state because of her father's stroke. If she really cared, don't you think she'd have shown up once or twice in the last few years?" He shook his head. "Cody, don't let a pretty face sway you. Stick with the Rocking F and let the Bar-B-Bar take care of itself."

"I know what I'm doing," Cody said.

He didn't need his brother telling him how to run his life.

"What about your work here?" Jarred asked.

"What about it. You have any cause for complaint?"

"No. But if you're trying to resurrect a dying ranch, how much time will you spend here?"

"No different than Tyler off chasing rodeos. You and Kyle can run things. I'll be around. It's not like the spread's halfway across the state. It's right next door. My home is here. Granted until I get the lay of the land, it might take up a lot of my time. We'll have to see."

"Because Tyler is off and gone and dad's on the cruise we're shorthanded."

"Give me a break. Granted at branding time or roundup, we can use every hand, but in the meantime, we've got a good crew. I'm done with this conversation."

Cody stood and walked off the porch.

He went the short distance to the cottage he called home. His brother could rile him up more than anyone. It was none of Jarred's business what Cody did—he was not the boss of him.

He turned on the TV and sank into the sofa, his feet going on the scarred coffee table. It was a moot point unless Holly took him up on his offer.

They'd had this argument the night before when he'd first broached the idea.

His grandfather wasn't opposed to it. That was good enough for Cody. It could work. He'd make sure of that.

9

The next morning Cody headed for the office. His father's philosophy was all his sons should understand all aspects of ranching, so they had each grown up taking on different tasks for a period of time. Cody didn't like paperwork. He'd rather be out on the range, but he had a good head for figures and often doubled checked his father's work when asked to do so.

Checking the latest batch of invoices against items purchased took most of the morning. Hadn't Jarred done anything last week? Probably not. He knew Cody had the best handle on accounting situations and probably let everything slide until Cody's turn.

The morning passed swiftly and by lunch time, Cody had caught up on all bills and receipts. The latest royalty check from the oil company had arrived and Cody processed the deposit slip. Next time he was in town, he'd take it to the bank.

When his father's father had first leased oil rights to the oil company, he'd set up a trust for his sons and grandchildren. The money was divided according to his original trust. The funds went a long way in keeping their ranch in tiptop condition despite the fluctuation in beef prices.

It also enabled Cody to have a bank account balance capable of buying another ranch or easily buying a partnership.

He sat back in the chair when he turned off the computer, thinking of Holly Braddock. He couldn't image his mother turning down a request for help from one of her children like Holly's mother had. But then, his parents were still happily married. Divorce was never good–but especially not for kids.

Carlos had sandwiches stacked on a plate in the middle of the table for those men who came in for lunch. Fruit, cookies and chips were also present in abundance as was iced tea.

Cody helped himself and sat down to eat. Three others straggled in, took their share and sat to eat.

"Anyone going to the dance at the Grange on Saturday," Pedro asked.

"I am," Carlos called from the kitchen.

"Me, too, Felipe said.

Pedro looked at Cody. "You?"

"Sure, wouldn't miss it."

He liked dancing, especially the slow songs when he could snug a woman up against him and enjoy the difference between men and women.

"You bringing the Braddock woman?" Carlos asked coming to the doorway and looking at Cody.

"Guess I could invite her. Let her get to meet her neighbors."

"Is she staying?" Felipe asked.

"Your guess is as good as mine," Cody said, wondering the same thing himself. He doubted it. But one never knew.

"It's a hot one again," Pedro said. "When I'm done work this afternoon, I'm heading for the swimming hole. I might stay there through supper, if I do, save me something, Carlos," he said.

"This isn't a restaurant, eat when it's supper time or not at all," Carlos said.

Everyone at the table knew his bark was worse than his bite. If one of the cowhands didn't show for supper, he'd save him a heaping plate.

Pedro grinned. "Thank you."

"I'm clearing out the water hole near pasture six after lunch" Felipe said. "It's a messy job, but someone's got to do it."

"Yeah, see how you feel if you get the assignment in February," Cody said.

He knew some water holes began to fill with weeds in the summer months and needed to be opened up for better access for the cows. And the cowboys doing that could get as wet as they wanted, which would sure help with the heat. He hoped it cooled down soon, days of endless high temperatures were beginning to wear on him.

He wondered how Holly was doing in the heat. Had she found another source of money? Still living with no power except for the generator? How long would she stay under such trying conditions?

Holly fed and watered the horses and thought about turning the hose on herself. It was so hot! The house was like an oven. It didn't cool down enough at night to cool the house and the heat built so fast each morning. The barn was a bit cooler, but not much.

Ever since Cody Fallon had made that tempting offer, she'd thought about little else. It'd go a long way to making things more tolerable on the ranch. She'd love a long hot soaking bath at the end of each day and a cool bedroom to sleep in at night.

She'd love not having to pull that cord to start the generator. Her shoulder ached continuously because of it.

There was work to be done and she was starting to realize she couldn't do it alone. She'd managed to saddle Starlight yesterday and even rode out to check on the cattle. But beyond finding some resting near the shade of a couple of trees, she didn't even find the main herd. Once again she wished for a map of the ranch so she'd have an idea of what she was supposed to be taking care of.

Today she'd corner her father's doctor and get some definite answers. No more being placated by he's making progress. She wanted to know what the reality of the stroke was. If he wasn't going to fully recover, she needed to know that now.

Dare she talk to her father about Cody's offer. Offers really—a loan or a buy in.

The loan would keep the ranch for her father. But could she ever pay it off?

Yet selling a partnership into the ranch seemed beyond what she could do to her father. How would he feel about it?

What would happen to the ranch if she didn't take Cody up on one of his offers?

She didn't want to think about that.

But as she leaned against the corral fence and felt it move, she knew she had to make a decision soon. For whatever reasons, the place needed major work. She couldn't do it as things were no matter how much she might wish she could.

Cody Fallon could do it. She expected he could do any and everything around a ranch. And do it well.

He was young, energetic and strong. Like her father had been before his stroke.

She went inside and washed in preparation of her visit. The doctor's prognosis would help her make a decision. She wished she was more knowledgeable about ranches and beef prices and cattle. Someone who could lay out the pros and cons she might not know about.

She'd talked to Brittany, but that California girl had no concrete suggestions, except for offering to lend Holly some money. Holly wouldn't hear of it. First of all she doubted Brit had enough for what she needed and there was the pay back she wasn't sure how to do until the ranch showed some profit.

Selling cattle still seemed her best bet.

Two hours later Holly was glad she'd visited with her father before talking with the doctor. She couldn't have hid her dismay around him. He was too astute.

She'd wanted a frank report from the doctor and got it in spades.

Driving through town, she stopped in front of Rosie's Café. A major infusion of caffeine would help. She felt she was in shock.

Carrie Sue was behind the counter chatting to two older cowboys. She smiled a welcome when Holly walked in.

"Table or counter?" she called.

"Counter's fine," Holly replied, taking a seat several spots away from the cowboys.

"Something to eat or just coffee?" Carrie Sue asked, setting a mug down in front of her.

"Give me the full breakfast," she said. "A granola bar for breakfast doesn't stick for long,"

"You've got it. Been to see your dad?" she asked, pouring the coffee.

She wrote the order down on a ticket and sent it back to the cook.

"Yes." Holly said, holding her mug like a lifeline. She took a small sip.

The coffee was hot, but tasted really good. She took another sip. How long before the caffeine began to perk her up?

"How's he doing?" Carrie Sue asked.

Holly stared at her for a moment then to her embarrassment burst into tears.

"Not good."

"Oh, honey, I'm so sorry," the waitress said, reaching across to grasp Holly's hand. "I thought he was getting better."

Holly nodded, taking a couple of napkins and blotting her cheeks and eyes.

"He is getting better, but the doctor said today he may never be the man he was before. He said he doesn't tell the patient that, since he doesn't want him to give up. Despite the therapy and all, his speech isn't coming back as much or as quickly as the doctor thought it should by this time. His coordination is off and there's definite weakness in the left side."

"But he'll still get better each day," Carrie Sue said encouragingly.

Holly nodded, crumpling the damp napkins in her hand.

"But I was counting on a full recovery and it doesn't look like that's going to happen."

"I'm sorry. I know that's a blow."

"I just don't know where to go from here. Do I save the ranch or sell it to fund whatever lifestyle my Dad might find when he leaves the hospital?"

"Oh, don't even think about selling the ranch. If there's one thing I've learned about ranchers it's the land means everything to them. There has to be another way to keep it so Frank will have his home when he leaves the hospital."

Holly thought of Cody's offers.

"Maybe," she said, taking another sip of coffee.

Her throat ached trying to keep the tears at bay. Life was so unfair. Her dad had done nothing to deserve this.

"Is there anything I can do?" Carrie Sue asked.

Holly shook her head.

"No, thanks for the offer. I appreciate it. I'll figure something out."

When her breakfast arrived she wasn't hungry. But not knowing when the next time she'd have a hot meal, She forced herself to eat. And gradually she felt marginally better.

The two cowboys left. Some others arrived and Carrie Sue was busy serving them.

"All done?" she asked Holly when she saw she'd finished eating."

"It was good. Thanks. I needed that."

"More coffee?"

"No, I need to get back to the ranch. Chores and all," she said.

"Maybe now's not the time to bring it up, but there's a

dance this Saturday night. At the Grange Hall. Come if you can. It'll be a good chance to meet people and take your mind off everything if only for a little while," Carrie Sue suggested.

Holly shook her head.

"I probably won't come but thanks for letting me know."

"It's at the Grange Hall behind the feed store. It starts at seven if you change your mind."

Holly climbed into the old truck desperately hoping for some amazing revelation that would make everything come right. But nothing changed. Her father was gravely ill. The ranch was still lacking basic care. And she was so tired of living with no electricity in this heat she considered bunking out in the barn.

The drive home gave her a chance to think about Cody. She hadn't seen him for two days. After his being around so much, she missed him. Had he given up on her? Was his offer of a loan still good?

"What if I make a partnership?" she asked aloud. "I could make stipulations that would protect my father, like the place would always be his home."

She thought about different conditions she'd like to see. Cody would probably have his own ideas. Was it even worth discussing?

"A loan would be better. If I sell enough cattle, I could pay him back. Then what," she continued. "If I spend all the money paying him back, I wouldn't have any left to carry through until the next sale. And if I sell all the cattle, there goes the livelihood. Darn it, Daddy why didn't you stop sending money you couldn't afford?"

She knew the answer to that.

Sighing, she turned into the drive that led to the house. It was so hot! She'd like to find a nice pool and sink up to her neck in cool water.

The ground reflected the heat as she checked the water in the trough. She couldn't stand around and do nothing.

Starlight ambled over to the corral fence and put her head over it, looking at Holly.

"You'd like to go for a ride, right?" she asked.

No time like the present to get further acquainted with the ranch. And it was too hot to do anything but sit on a horse and explore.

The saddle was hard to get on but she did it, feeling a small sense of triumph. Getting on was easy if she used the bottom rail of the corral.

She learned from her first ride with Cody and had her own hat, and long sleeves even though the temperature had to be approaching a hundred. No more sunburn for her.

Aiming Starlight toward the left of the house, she surveyed the land as they walked. It was dry, as she remembered from her visits before. Yet there was plenty of grass for grazing. That was good.

When they reached a fence, she had Starlight walk along side of it until they reached a gate. It was closed. For a moment, Holly considered dismounting to open it, but wasn't sure she could get back up on the horse. Something to practice back at the house, not so far away in case she couldn't get back up.

They followed the fence until she spotted a clump of trees. Beneath the trees were a dozen or more cattle, seeking whatever shade they could.   She headed that way. She remembered summers in the past when she'd ride the range with her dad. Why hadn't she learned more from those days?

One of the cattle was off to one side. When she got closer she could see a tangle of barbed wire around its left leg. She remembered Cody saying always be prepared for anything. She didn't have any wire cutters, but could she unwind the wire? The injury looked days old. The cuts were no longer bleeding but were muddy scabs.

There was no help for it, she had to dismount. That was the easy part. She'd worry about the rest later.

She tied the horse to one of the trees and walked slowly to the injured cow.

"Easy, there," she crooned.

Some of the cows rose to their feet and ambled away from her. The injured one stared at her with large brown eyes.

"I want to help," she said softly as she approached. She hoped she could get the wire off and not make things worse.

The cow remained lying down. Could it sense she wanted to help?

Reaching out her hand, she tried to find a spot between the barbs to grasp. Working slowly, crooning the whole while, she unwrapped it from the leg. The cow didn't move.

Finally she had the wire off. Trying to coil it so it couldn't injure any other animals, she cut her hands twice.

Definitely next up for her was a pair of strong leather gloves. She didn't know what to do with the wire when done. Should she take it home or leave it somewhere? Where, though, that another steer wouldn't get tangled?

Taking it home seemed the best option.

She looked around hoping to spy a mound or something

that would make it easier for her to mount the horse. The land gradually sloped upward, but not steep enough to help her.

She couldn't mount holding the wire. Yet she didn't have saddle bags or anything to put it in. Finally she wedged it between a tree trunk and first branch. She'd be able to reach it from the horse, she thought.

It took ten minutes and Holly was drenched with perspiration when she finally reached her seat in the saddle. She had to find a better way. For a moment she considered riding with a stool. Wouldn't that give cowboys a laugh. Not that there were any around to see.

Urging Starlight to the tree, she was able to get the wire, cutting her finger again.

The sooner she got home and washed the better. She didn't want to get gangrene or something from the dirty wire.

She wasn't sure of the way back, so gave Starlight her head. She knew the horse would return to her food supply.

Sure enough in less than an hour, Holly reached the barn. She unsaddled the horse, brushed some of her damp hide and turned her loose in the corral. Checking the water again, she was pleased to see there was enough to last until the afternoon feeding.

Heading for the house, she hoped she'd filled all the sinks. She wanted to wash the cuts and apply antiseptics.

Once done, she sat out on the back steps staring at the barn. Everything she saw only emphasized how lacking she was in being able to keep this place for her dad. Maybe it was time to talk to Cody.

She hoped he hadn't changed his mind.

She climbed into the truck and headed for town. She needed cell service and there wasn't any at the ranch.

When she saw she had enough bars, she pulled over and called the Rocking F.

Seth answered the phone.

"It's Holly Braddock, is Cody there?"

"He's out and about, Holly, can I help you?'

"No, thanks. I, uh, wanted to talk to Cody. Do you expect him back soon?"

"He'll be in for supper. That's about all I can count on," Seth said with some humor. "You doing all right?"

"Yes."

Not at all, but she didn't want to burden Seth Johnson.

"Your dad coming along?" he asked.

"As the doctor expects," she said, trying not to remember every single detail the man had laid out for her—at her own insistence. That would teach her to want to face facts.

"I expect we'll be talking with my son soon. He'll be unhappy to hear the news about your dad's stroke. He and Frank are good friends. You'll let us know if you need anything, right?"

She hesitated a moment. Maybe this was the answer to her questions.

"There is one thing, if you could give me some advice," she said.

Would Seth be an impartial man to talk to, or would he favor Cody over all?

"What's that?"

She took a deep breath.

"I had a lengthy talk with the doctor today. His long term prognosis for my dad's recovery isn't good. The doctor doesn't think he'll be up to ranching again."

She clamped down hard on her emotions. She would not cry again. Time for solutions, not mourning.

"I'm right sorry to hear that. Frank loves his ranch."

"I know. I want to do whatever I can to keep it for him. Uh, Cody offered a couple of things that could help. A loan or an offer to buy into the ranch and be a partner. I wondered if you had any feelings on what would be a better solution, both short term and long term."

"That's hard to say. Depends on the terms of each, I'd think. And depends on what you want. I know Frank will want to go home when he's recovered enough to leave the convalescent hospital, however much he does recover. Will you be there? Or would it be better to have a partner to run things and let Frank know someone else with knowledge and experience will be running things for them both?"

"So it depends on me," she said.

Right now this moment she wanted to save the ranch at all costs. But could she stay? Her mother had not been able to. For years she'd heard her mother complain about ranch life.

But Holly wasn't her mother. So far she'd seen nothing to turn her away from staying. She deserved some time with her father since most of her life had been spent with her mother.

And there was something about the land that called to her. Was that in her blood? Her father's family had owned this land for generations. If it didn't go to her, was it to go to strangers upon his death?

Or to a partner who loved the land and made it flourish?

"I need to talk to Cody," she said. "Tell him I'm ready to talk business."

"I'll tell him as soon as I see him," Seth said.

"Thank you. And I think your comments have helped clarify things for me."

Holly spent the rest of the afternoon near the house in case Cody showed up.

She started the generator again to water the horses.

She tried to make sense out of the paperwork in her father's office, but except for stacking bills in order of due dates, and tallying the total, she didn't understand the other records and invoices.

By dinner time, Cody still hadn't come by. Had he changed his mind? She hoped not. Eating a peanut butter and jelly sandwich for dinner, Holly also took a quick shower while the generator kept the water flowing. There was no hot water, but with the house so warm, she relished the cold water.

She'd never take electricity for granted again. Her cuts stung a little and she applied more ointment on them when she dried off.

She was about to give up on hearing from Cody when she heard his truck in the driveway.

He'd come.

Walking out, she watched him get out of his truck and walk toward her. The light was fading, but it was clear enough to see the man. He didn't look like a white knight, but he did look solid, strong, capable. And somewhat determined.

Just what was needed.

As long as she could hold her own against him.

"Granddad said you wanted to see me," he said when he was close enough to touch.

She swallowed. It was do or die time.

"I did, do. I want to talk partnership."

10

Cody nodded. "Okay, let's do it."

"Do you want to come inside? I have to warn you it's hot as can be inside."

"I reckon we can sit out."

"There's a swing and some chairs on the front porch. I used to swing there a lot when I was a kid," she said, stepping off the back stoop and walking around the side of the house.

Cody matched her steps. When they reached the porch he sat on one of the chairs. She chose the swing.

"So, what made you decide to go for my offer?" he asked.

"Didn't you talk to your grandfather?"

"He said at dinner you wanted to see me. Why?"

"I thought he might have told you. I had a long discussion with the doctor today. My dad's never going to be back the way he was. The doctor wasn't sure if he'd ever walk without a walker. Wasn't sure he'd be able to talk properly and sure didn't think he'd have the stamina to run a ranch."

He watched her closely, seeing tears form again. He hoped she wouldn't cry. It made him feel so inept when women cried.

She took a deep breath.

"I want him to live here until he dies. He could live another forty or fifty years, and I want him to be in the home he loves."

"Sure."

"So that would be a stipulation."

Cody nodded. He expect some negotiations. He'd thought about it for several days now. He wasn't entirely sure of his own motives for wanting this. To help out Frank, of course. And Holly. To have something of his own away from his family was part of it.

"And I'd want to be here, too, helping," she said.

He cocked his head slightly. "Help how?"

"However I can. I'm my dad's sole heir. I'm assuming he'd leave me the ranch. I need to know how to run it."

"I can run it."

"Partners, remember? I want to learn."

"It can be really hard work."

"I know. And from some of the things you've said, this place needs a lot of it. I want to be part of bringing it back to being a successful working ranch."

"I figured you'd take off for California."

"Not going to happen."

He wasn't totally sure about that.

Either way, it wouldn't matter. He'd have a stake in another ranch beside the Rocking F. It was a start.

"Okay, let's talk terms."

They discussed the terms of the partnership. Cody was surprised when Holly suggested they consult her father's attorney to lay out everything in partnership papers. He'd thought he'd have to be the one to suggest that.

"How much are you planning to invest?" she asked.

"We'll get the place appraised and I'll put up enough to cover fifty percent."

"Forty-nine percent," she countered. "I want my dad to have the majority."

He shook his head. "Fifty-fifty. Until Frank is up and around again, I'm in charge. You don't know enough to run it and I don't want to have to argue with you over any decision I make."

She thought a moment. "What about if in a year my dad wants to buy one percent, giving him fifty-one percent, you go for that."

Cody nodded. "Okay, I'll agree to that. But only Frank can make that decision, not someone who has his power of attorney."

"Me, you mean"

"Got it in one," he said with a grin.

Excitement began to build. He could already think of half a dozen things he'd do immediately. To see the result of his work, really pulling the ranch out of the morass it was in to making it a success, made him all the more ready to start.

"One more thing. Don't tell my father. I want to tell him. I want to wait a little while to see how things go with his rehab. I'm afraid he'll give up if he thinks someone else is running the ranch. I know his desire to get home is fueling some of his effort at therapy."

"Fine by me. What happened to your hands?" he asked.

"I went out riding today and found a cow tangled in barbed wire. I had to get it off. Nasty stuff, barbed wire."

"You need gloves."

"I'm learning as I go. I definitely will pick up a pair the next time I'm in town."

"Which will be tomorrow. I'll pick you up at nine. Call for

an appointment with the attorney, then we'll head for the bank, then the electric company in that order."

She grinned. "Sounds good to me. I can't wait to cool off the house. Is it always this hot here?"

"Nope, in winter we get snow."

"I've never been here in winter," she said wistfully.

"You'll be wishing for this heat when you're out slogging in the slush trying to get feed to cattle because the snow's too deep for grazing."

"Too bad we can't even out the weather."

"That'd be a treat."

He stood. "I'll see you in the morning."

"Okay. Thank you, Cody."

He stepped off the porch and started for his truck. Then he stopped and looked back at her. Speaking before he even thought it through, he said, "There's a dance at the Grange on Saturday. Want to go? It'll be a good chance to meet more of your neighbors."

"Carrie Sue told me about it. I said no to her, but now that I've made up my mind to stay, maybe I should meet some other neighbors."

"I'll pick you up at six-thirty on Saturday, and nine tomorrow."

He wondered why he'd blurted out the invitation as he drove back home. Granted it would be a good opportunity for Holly to meet others from the area. Most of the ranching community went to Grange events from ranchers to cowboys to town people.

But he rarely invited anyone to go with him. He remembered the time he'd invited Debbie Robinson. The town gossip had them engaged before they left that night. Even Debbie had gotten the wrong idea.

Or maybe she'd started listening to the gossip that ran rampant.

Until the next Fallon boy took a girl to a Grange dance.

That'd been Kyle. He remembered the horror Kyle shared when he was linked to Bessie McConnell. They'd hardly spoken since then.

Not that there was anything romantic about taking Holly Braddock. Everyone would know that. They'd just met. She was here for her father. Frank was well liked, so everyone would be nice to her for his sake.

Cody knew every cowboy in town would be interested in her. She was pretty enough for anyone to be captivated. Not that it had anything to do with him. Their relationship was purely business.

Yet the thought of other cowboys making a play for her at the dance rubbed him the wrong way.

His grandfather came out of the barn when Cody drove into the yard. He headed for the truck.

"You talk to that girl?" Seth asked.

"Yeah, we're going to see Frank's attorney in the morning," Cody said, getting out of the truck and putting on his hat.

"Then I'll be half owner of the Bar-B-Bar. No matter what Jarred says, I don't think Holly's going to leave. Might be wrong, but she strikes me as being pigheaded enough to stay and see it through. She's mighty attached to her father."

"Jarred's cynical, you know that. And you can't blame him for his views about Holly. Frank has nearly bankrupted the place to keep her living high."

"I don't think she knew. I mean, yeah he sent money to fund everything she wanted, but I don't think she thought it was a hardship. In fact, I'm worried when she finds out, she'll really freak. But I think her mom knew. And wrung every cent from him she could, through guilt or whatever."

"I remember Adrienne. She was so out of place here. I believe at the time she thought she'd be like some of the Hollywood set which owns fancy ranches to visit once or twice a year and throw lavish parties. The realities of ranching isn't for everyone."

"No matter, once I'm officially a partner, any payments to her stops. Unless it was mandated in the divorce decree. I'd want to check that out as well."

"You've got a good head on your shoulders, Cody. Just take it slowly."

"Yeah, I know. I'm not going to risk all I've saved over the years on a venture I don't feel I can control. But Frank has prime grazing land and plenty of wells for water. His cattle should be thriving."

"You'll do a lot of good for the Braddocks," Seth said as they began walking to the bunkhouse.

"Jarred's going to put up a stink, isn't he," Cody asked.

"You know your brother. No one knows as much as he does."

"In his own mind, maybe. Anyway, keep this on the QT if you would, until it's a done deal. I don't want him arguing with me all night long."

"You know what you're doing," Seth said.

The men had already finished dinner, but cook had kept a plate for Cody. His grandfather sat with him as he ate.

"What's the going rate for buying into property these days?" Seth asked.

"Haven't a clue. We're setting it up that I buy into half, after it's appraised. Now I'm wondering if the appraisal will come in low since the place is falling down. Honestly for a smart rancher, Frank let things go all for his daughter. What makes a man do that?"

"Love of that daughter and proving to the ex-wife that he was someone she shouldn't have left, I expect," Seth said.

He rose and poured himself a cup of coffee and sat again.

"Always trying to prove to Adrienne that he could keep her and their daughter in the lifestyle she wanted. Foolishness, but men do that when in love."

"He's in love with his ex?" Cody said, startled.

"Could be. Could merely be a habit by now. I don't know the man as well as your father does. Ask him."

"It doesn't matter. He could have been close to dying and all that ex of his wanted was for Holly to come home. No love loss on her end."

"How's Holly holding up."

"I thought she'd start crying at one point. I hate it when women cry," Cody said. "She's looking out for her dad, though. She wants him to be able to change the terms of the agreement in a year if he's capable."

"What agreement?" Jarred asked, entering the dining room.

Cody looked up, taking the last bite of the stew.

"Nothing that concerns you."

"You're going ahead with an offer for half the Bar-B-Bar, aren't you? I told you it's a stupid move. You'll be saddled with a failing ranch and no help to be found but what you fund. Don't do it, bro."

Cody shrugged. He and Jarred had gone head to head a couple of nights ago about his idea of buying into the ranch. Nothing since then had changed his mind, nor his brother's. This was one area they had to agree to disagree.

"Stubborn idiot," Jarred said.

He sat beside his grandfather.

"Talk some sense into him."

"He's grown. Doesn't need me chiming in."

"And some men learn everything the hard way," Jarred said. "What about your work on our ranch?"

"It's not like there's life or death stuff to do. We have plenty of hands. I'll pull my weight, but might take a few days off to get things going on the Bar-B-Bar. You have a problem with that?"

"Only that you're heading for a fall and I hate to see it."

"Time will tell, Jarred. I think I can pull it off."

"I think you're not thinking but letting your emotions cloud the issues. She's pretty, I grant you. But Holly has nothing going for her here. She doesn't know ranching, knows nothing about cattle. What she does know is parties and flitting around. How long do you think it'll be before she takes off?"

Cody shrugged. He wasn't going to let his brother know he had his own doubts about Holly staying. He could manage without her. And maybe he should write something into the agreement that she stays for at least that year time frame she wanted for her father to buy back one percent.

"I've got it handled."

"Time will tell," Jarred said.

Holly drove into town after supper. She needed to talk to someone about her decision and her best friend was her first choice always. She parked near the park at the heart of town and went to sit on one of the benches. The heat was fading and by dark it would probably be cool enough to enjoy herself. She quickly dialed Brittany hoping she was home.

"Hi Holly, what's up?" Brittany answered right away.

"Just needed a friend. Got a few minutes."

"Sure do. How's your dad?"

"Not so good." Holly updated her friend on the future possibilities of her father's recovery. "Which is why I've made a decision. But now that I've started things in motion, I'm worried I'm making a mistake. I wish I could discuss this with my dad, but I don't want to get him worried or upset which this might do."

"What might do?"

"I'm taking on a partner for the ranch."

Brittany was silent for a moment. "What does that mean?"

"It means there will be someone there who knows how to run a ranch, show me the ropes and keep it going until my dad gets better. Only it doesn't sound as if he's going to get all the way back to where he was. We may end up selling the ranch and my father would live off the proceeds."

"Wow, that's a big change. Do you think your dad would approve?"

"Not if he was in good health. He's run that place by himself since his father died. The ranch has been in the family for three generations. I hate to be the one to end that record, but I know nothing about ranching and am not sure how much I want to learn. But it's his life."

"If he can't do it anymore, then you have to make the hard decisions," Brit said. "Who's buying in and how did you get an offer so soon?"

"It was his idea. Cody Fallon, a cowboy from the ranch next to dad's. He brought the idea up. At first I said no, but the longer I thought about it, it does make sense. And I'm trying to make sure dad can buy him out in the future if things turn out better than thought right now."

"Isn't Cody the one you told me about?"

"Yes."

Holly tried to remember what she'd told her best friend. Surely not how fascinated she was by him. She was there for her father, not to develop some crush on a cute cowboy. One who didn't hold her in very high regard.

"The other thing is, I've been going through my dad's records, and I think I'm the reason the ranch is in such bad shape."

"How could you be, you haven't been there in years."

"I know, but in looking over records for the last few years, he's taking out loans from the bank, and put off some repairs and things to fund my college and then my trip to Europe. I had no idea he didn't have tons of money. My mother always said there was no worries over money from my dad. He didn't have to do any of it. Once I turned eighteen, wasn't his obligation satisfied?"

"I have no idea. My guess is he wanted to do that for you."

"To the detriment of his own livelihood. Doesn't make sense to me. Anyway, now I have that added development haunting me. If the ranch is in bad shape because I was flitting around Europe, it's up to me to make it right."

"You and Cody."

"Yeah, me and the cowboy."

"He's cute."

"How do you know that?" Holly asked.

Had she told Brittany how she felt around the man?

"Just assuming. Aren't all cowboys cute. What's he like."

"Masculine with a capital M. He has the most gorgeous blue eyes. Actually they all do."

"All who?"

"The Fallon men."

"Oh, there's more than one? And you've met them all? Do tell."

"I was invited to dinner a couple of times. There are four brothers, but one's out doing rodeos somewhere. Their grandfather lives on the ranch, too, and he also has those blue eyes."

"Eyes. What else?"

"Tall, over six feet–all of them. Built, but not like a body builder, just muscular from ranch work, I guess. And he sits on a horse like they are melded together."

"Okay, you've lost me here. You're riding horses?"

"Yes. It's a ranch. That's how we ride out to check on things."

"Oh, girl, that's so foreign to me. And you like it? Don't horses smell?"

"They have a horsey smell, but remember I used to spend my summers here. I love the smell of horses, fresh hay, sage, even dirt here in Wyoming. I should have been here every summer. I'd know more about running a cattle ranch if I'd kept up my visits."

"If you get this cowboy running things, are you coming home?"

"No. I'm staying here."

"Forever?"

Holly gazed across the park. In the distance she could see rolling hills, dotted with trees and grass. There was a soft breeze playing across her face bring in the scents that only Wyoming produced. A peace pervaded.

"I might."

"Oh, girl, I'm coming out there to talk sense into you. There's no way you can spend your life in Wyoming. You're a California girl through and through."

Holly laughed. "You would be a fish out of water here, Brittany, but I really like it. We'll see how the next few weeks go. Do you think I'm doing the right thing selling part of the ranch? I hate to abuse my power of attorney."

"You have that for a reason. It's because your father can't cope right now. He trusts you to do what's needed. I say you're doing the right thing. Keep the ranch going until you know for certain what your dad's limitations might be. Future decisions can be made in the future. Go for it, girl."

"Thanks."

"Did you hear from your mother?"

"No. The phone doesn't work at the house and I don't get cell service there. I'm in town now to talk to you. I didn't even check messages. She's probably called a dozen times."

"You're in charge, remember that. And ask her what she'd want you to do for her if she were in a similar situation."

Holly laughed again. "I'd be waiting on her hand and foot. She holds such animosity for my father. How did they ever fall in love and get married?"

"Hormones, most likely. Anyway, glad it happened however it did since their marriage produced you. Who would I have as a BFF if you weren't around?"

"Joyce Hancock?"

Brittany laughed at the mention of a women neither of them could stand. "Right."

"Thanks for being here for me, Brittany. I have to go now to call the attorney to see if he can meet with us tomorrow. I'll call you after we meet and let you know how it goes."

Holly arranged a meeting at ten the next day, explaining the basics of what she wanted. To her surprise, he was in total agreement with the idea. Once the three of them met, he'd be able to draw up a contract and finalize the deal.

She drove through the local drive in for an ice cream before heading back to the ranch. It was not full dark when she drove home. She needed light to see where to turn into the driveway. The house couldn't be seen from the road, not that it had any lights on to begin with. That would change once the partnership was established.

Holly hoped thing would work out and she wasn't making the biggest mistake of her life.

Cody was shaving the next morning when his brother Kyle pounded on the door. "Mom and Dad are on Skype. Come on down as quick as you can,"

"Be there in a minute." Cody quickly finished, rinsed his face and headed for the office where the big monitor was.

Kyle, Jarred and Carlos were standing behind Seth who was seated in the desk chair.

"Here's Cody," Seth said.

"Hey Mom, Dad. How are things going?"

Cody stepped into view of the camera.

"Great," his mother answered.

"We are having the best time. And we've met some people from Colorado who we like a lot. It makes meal time fun to visit with them."

"Everything okay there?" his dad asked.

Seth shook his head. "Fine on the ranch, but Frank Braddock had a stroke."

"Oh no, how is he, Dad?" Marge asked.

"In rehab now. But progress is slow."

"Not expected to fully recover," Cody added.

"That bad. What's happening at his place?" his father asked.

"His daughter's there."

"Holly?" John asked. "I remember her from when she was a little girl. She hasn't visited in years."

"Is she coping all right?" his mother asked.

"We've got it covered," Cody said.

He stepped out of camera range and nailed Jarred with a look. Shaking his head, he hoped he conveyed he did not want his plans shared.

Jarred nodded once.

"What?" their mother asked, picking up on Jarred's nod.

"Agreeing with Cody that the ranch is being covered. Neighbors do that after all, didn't you hammer that into us as kids?" Jarred said easily.

"I never hammered anything," their mother protested.

Every one of the Fallon men laughed. Marge might not

think so, but she had a way of making sure her sons knew her values and followed them.

"How is cruise life, still exciting? You've been gone a month, I'd be tired of seeing so much ocean," Seth said.

"I, personally, love it. Not to live on the sea all the time, but for this trip, it's fabulous," she said. "We've been really lucky with wonderful weather."

"It's hot here, Mom," Kyle said. "And fire danger is rising."

Cody moved back into camera range. His brother was a volunteer firefighter and could be counted on to always know the fire danger in the surrounding area.

It still seemed odd to have his parents half a world away. But a cruise was something they had wanted to do for a long time and what better time to do it than when their sons were grown and they were still young enough to enjoy the experience.

When the call ended, the men lounged around on the various chairs and sofa in the office. Seth leaned back in the desk and looked around.

"Might as well hold a family council," he said.

Jarred laughed.

"Yeah, like we need that. What's up?"

"I thought Cody should bring everyone up to date on his situation."

"What situation?" Kyle asked.

Carlos looked at Cody.

Cody scowled at his grandfather.

"Had to bring it up again," he murmured.

"What?" Kyle asked.

"Tell him, Cody. I'd be interested to see if he views it the same way," Jarred said, stretching his long legs out and slouching back in the leather chair.

"Someone tell me," Kyle said.

"I'm buying into the Bar-B-Bar," Cody said shortly, giving Jarred a challenging look.

"Why?"

"To play white knight to a damsel in distress," Jarred murmured.

"No," Cody replied quickly. "It's a business decision. The ranch is falling apart and the latest prognosis from the doctors is that Frank is never going to be the man he was. There will be limitations. The only question is what and how bad. He can't even talk."

"So why buy into a failing ranch?" Kyle asked.

"Especially with a pretty woman there," Jarred inserted. "Though for how long?"

"That's enough, Jarred," Seth said. "Let Cody tell it."

"I know as well as you do that it's highly unlikely Holly will stay. She hasn't a clue about ranching. She hasn't even visited in ten years, since she was a young teenager. Right now she's concerned about her dad. But once Frank is stabilized, and the truth of his situation is realized by all involved, I figure she'll sell out the other half. And who better to sell it to than the half owner. The property's right next to ours, increasing our overall size if Frank sells. And if he doesn't, then I still have half interest with a clause allowing him to buy me out in the future at the then going market value."

Kyle studied his brother for a minute then nodded. "Makes sense."

"No it doesn't," Jarred said, sitting up. "First the place is falling apart. So not only is there the work needed to get it back operating in the black, there's a lot of fix up which will take extra time and money. That would all be on Cody. Which means he's not going to be much help around here."

"I can still pull my weight," Cody protested.

"We have enough hands to keep going, Jarred. If things get tight, call Tyler home from the rodeo circuit. We can manage. I think it's a good idea," Kyle said.

Cody smiled. At least he had Kyle on his side. And, with a quick glance at his grandfather, he knew he had Seth's approval as well.

"Face it bro, you wished you'd thought of it first," Cody said.

Jarred shook his head and stood.

"I think you are throwing good money after bad. And you'll kill yourself trying to work two ranches at once. Once the pretty face is gone, I expect the venture to lose its appeal."

He turned and left the room.

"She is pretty," Kyle said. "But even better if she leaves, then any decisions you make wouldn't be up for discussion. You are going to have controlling interest, right?"

"Fifty-fifty," Cody said.

"Let's hope she acknowledges that you know a might more about ranching than she does and lets you call the shots."

"That's my plan."

"Count me in to help out if I can."

"Me, too," Carlos added.

He rose and said he had to get back to the bunkhouse to finish breakfast.

Kyle watched as their long-time hand left.

"Your plan sure got Jarred riled up. Why?" he asked.

Cody shrugged and looked at his grandfather. "Any ideas?"

"I expect the boy's cynicism is coming through. He was burned pretty badly by Sheila Dunn if you recall. He doesn't trust women much, especially those who depend on others to support them in the style they like. I don't see that with Holly. I can't say if she has what it takes to stick it out, but I don't think she's taking you for a ride."

11

Cody drove to the Bar-B-Bar early to help with feeding the horses. He had a list of things to get for the Rocking F when in town. He didn't plan to give Jarred any room for complaint.

He checked the water tank, then headed for the pump house to get the generator going. He hoped he could clear up the electric bill and get the power back on today.

The roar of the generator filled the air. He returned to the barn and fed the horses, giving some carrots he'd brought to each of them for a treat. When the tank was full, he considered shutting off the generator, but figured Holly could use the power at the house.

He was about to go knock on the door when she appeared, looking like she just woke up.

"Cody? What are you doing here so early?"

"Got things to do. Were you still sleeping?"

She nodded, then walked across the dirt to join him.

"Guess I need to get up earlier, right?"

He looked at the sky. "The best time of the day is before it gets too hot to want to move. Did you reach the attorney?"

He hoped she hadn't changed her mind.

"Yes. He can see us at ten. And he thinks it's a good idea."

Cody nodded. "Do you need a ride into town or shall I meet you there?"

"Meet me there, you know where the attorney's office is?"

"Sure do."

"I'm going in early to see my dad. Once we get things settled, I'll be ready to do whatever is needed to get going. I'm buying leather gloves and a sturdier hat. Anything else I need?"

He looked at her feet clad in sandals. Dirt already dusting her toes.

"You have boots, are they comfortable? You'll be in them a lot."

"Yes they're comfortable. And I have jeans. All set, then."

"Some long sleeve shirts so you don't get burned. And a bathing suit."

"A bathing suit?"

She looked surprised at that.

"We've got a nice swimming hole on the ranch, Wildcat Creek runs through a corner, and the water's really cool on hot days. You might want to go swimming with the rest of us."

She hadn't brought a bathing suit. She'd thought she might even be too late to see him alive. But since she was staying for the foreseeable future, she'd pick one up.

"Thanks for taking care of the horses. I'll get up earlier tomorrow."

"Okay. I'll take off then. See you at ten."

Holly watched him drive away and turned back to the house. She hoped she was up to life on a ranch. Up before the sun, bed at sundown? She'd probably be tired enough.

"Good morning, Dad," Holly said entering her father's room a few minutes after eight. "How are you feeling today?"

"Be..er," he struggled to say. "You?"

"Doing great. I'm buying some things I didn't bring with me today, like a bathing suit. Cody Fallon told me there's a swimming hole on their ranch and he invited me to join them swimming some time. I met the rest of the family. Well, except his parents and there's one more brother, Tyler, whom I haven't met. The three brothers I met sure do look alike. And like their grandfather."

"Annn mmmm–"

"And their mother?"

Frank nodded frustration evident in his expression.

"I hear you and John Fallon are great friends, at least that's the way the Fallon men tell it."

Frank nodded. "Loonngg–"

"Long time?"

He nodded.

Holly wanted to steer the conversation away from the ranch in case her dad had questions about how things were going. She decided not to mention the debt the ranch was in due to her year in Europe, but she could give him a recap, show she'd learned so much that maybe he'd think it worth it in the long run. Especially when she planned to make it up to him by staying on the ranch and with Cody's knowledge, make it a success again.

"This morning's sunrise reminded me of one I saw in Provence," she began.

Soon she was regaling him about her time in each of the European countries she visited. She could tell by the ways his eye lit that he was pleased to hear of how much she'd relished each new experience.

He grew tired sooner than Holly would have liked. But she'd stop by on her way home for a quick visit. Giving him a kiss, she told him to rest up until the physical therapist arrived.

Shopping didn't take long. It was ten minutes to ten when she arrived at the attorney's office. She entered, wanting to wait in air-conditioned comfort rather than in the hot truck.

"He'll be with you shortly," the receptionist said with a smile. "Can I get you anything while you wait? Tea? Coffee?"

"No, thanks."

Five minutes later Cody Fallon strode in. He glanced around and saw Holly and went to sit beside her.

"Oh, Cody, I didn't know you're meeting with Bart," the receptionist said. "Do you have an appointment?"

"I'm with Holly," he said.

She looked at Holly then back at Cody, her expression priceless.

Holly didn't laugh, but couldn't help a smile. The girl obviously had a crush on Cody.

She glanced at the man sitting beside her. He held his hat in his hands, slowly turning it round and round. His jeans were clean. Even his boots looked like they were the dress-up kind, not scuffed or worn. He even smelled clean and fresh, like the fields of Wyoming.

Her heart skipped a beat and she looked away. They were here on business, nothing more.

The door behind the receptionist's desk opened and an older woman beckoned. "Come on back, Bart's free now.

Holly led the way, conscious of Cody only a couple of

steps behind her. She could almost feel the heat of his body. Which made her own temperature rise.

Thankfully the visitor chairs in the attorney's office were not close together. She needed the breathing room.

Cody let her outline their plan, only inserting a clarification here and there. Both agreed to the terms as Bart jotted them down.

"Sounds straightforward. I can draft up the preliminary agreement in the next day or two. Ready to sign when you have the appraisal of the ranch and agree on the amount."

Cody nodded.

Holly agreed. She glanced at Cody.

"You can have the money ready that soon?"

He nodded again.

Holly was impressed. She didn't know how much the ranch was worth, but she didn't know anyone who had that kind of money readily available.

When they left together, Cody stopped her on the sidewalk.

"I set up a new bank account for this joint venture. We'll run income and expenses through it and not mingle funds for each of us. I'll start it off with a few thousand dollars and once we have the appraisal, we can decide how much we want to use as working capital. The rest can go into your father's account."

"Okay."

"You need to go to the bank to sign the card so they have your signature on file."

"I'll be signing checks, too?"

"We're partners. The account is for the ranch."

She was surprised he'd thought of that. It made sense.

"I can do that now."

"Good. Then we'll head for the electric company, the phone company and the grocery store. Did you get your other shopping done?" he asked as he walked beside her to her truck.

"I did. I'm ready to head home when we're finished."

"I'll ride with you. When we're done, you can drop me off at my truck," he said, opening the driver door for her.

The bank officer was ready for Holly and she quickly signed the appropriate forms to have access to the joint account.

Errands after took the better part of an hour.

"Want to eat lunch before buying groceries?" Cody asked.

He was hungry and thought she might be as well. It was just before noon, but hours since he ate breakfast.

"Sure."

"Rosie's okay with you?"

"Yes. Is there any other place?"

"Just the drive-in for hamburgers or a fancy restaurant."

Carrie Sue greeted them from behind the counter when they entered the café a few minutes later. It was not yet noon, so there were still plenty of open tables. Cody chose one near the window and Carrie Sue came to take their order.

"What brings you two to town?" she asked as she set glasses of water on the table.

"Shopping," Cody said.

Holly reached for the water and took a sip. So he wasn't making their agreement known just yet. Interesting.

They ordered and Carrie Sue greeted another set of customers as they entered.

"It'll get crowded in a few minutes," Cody said. "Glad we got here early."

"I've eaten here several times. The food's good and the prices are really low."

"Harry's run this place for years. It was a hangout when my folks were dating."

"Carrie Sue can't have been here that long, she doesn't seem old enough to have been employed but a few years."

"Actually, she's Harry's granddaughter. Has worked here off and on for I don't know, maybe eight years. Maybe longer. She worked through high school. Then went off to college. When her grandmother died, she came home to help Harry with the place. Been here ever since."

"She has an interest in travel, I see," Holly said, nodding toward the back wall which was plastered in postcards from all over the world.

"Yeah. She and Phillip Parker have been a couple since they were in high school. He's some foreign news correspondent. Hasn't been home in years as I recall. But he sends her cards from wherever he is."

"That's interesting. Long distance relationships don't usually work very well for long."

"Yeah, well Carrie Sue seems content, so I guess it's working okay. I've never heard her say she wants to travel."

"I recognize some of the locations on the postcards," Holly said. "I could see them better when I sat at the counter."

"I bet you do. You spent enough time in Europe to see everything."

She looked at Cody.

"What do you mean by that?"

She was super sensitive to the situation of her father's spending so much for her year abroad.

He met her gaze his eyes narrowing slightly.

"I meant you were there a year, I expect you saw most of Europe."

"I didn't know it was a financial hardship on my dad," she said quickly.

He studied her a moment. "I never said anything about that."

She looked away.

"I found out since I've been here. Dad had no business financing anything so extravagant. I didn't know it would about bankrupt the ranch."

"He made his own decisions. Not up to us to second guess him," Cody said.

She met his gaze again.

"Easy for you to say, you didn't take all that money and never once ask where it came from or was it taking away from something else. This ranch is his life. What is he going to do if he can't keep it?"

"He's going to keep it. I'm just buying into it, not taking over. We'll let the future take care of itself."

Cody didn't know how to answer her. Her family dynamics were a mess. Nothing like his family, so he hadn't a clue how to deal with it.

"We can't change the past. But we can make the future strong," he offered.

"I want to pull my weight. You'll have to teach me stuff, but I can learn."

He nodded. "If you stay."

"What do you mean if I stay. I'm here aren't I?"

"For how long? Working a ranch is nothing like visiting museums in foreign countries. It's hot, sweaty, hard work a lot of the time. Other times, it's downright boring. Or we're slogging about in mud freeing a cow stuck in a mud hole. Or dealing with the stench of branding and castrating that you think will never go away."

"There may be things I can't do, but I'll try anything once. And get rid of the idea I'm leaving any time soon. I neglected my dad for years. Time to make up for that. I'm staying."

Cody shrugged. He had his doubts. Time would tell.

"I am!" Holly said firmly.

Carrie Sue arrived with their food and for a few minutes there was silence at their table as they began to eat. When the first pangs of hunger were satisfied, Holly asked, "How are you going to be able to work on the Bar-B-Bar if you have work on your family ranch?"

"I'll shift things around. Jarred isn't too happy with me right now. Too bad. We have enough ranch hands working to keep things going even with me, Tyler and my dad gone."

"That's three cowboys who could be doing work. Doesn't that put a burden on the others who are there?"

"Probably not much right now. When it's time for all hands on deck, I'll be there. Same as they'll rally around if we need help on the Bar-B-Bar. One of the first things we'll do is hire at least a couple of other cowboys, three more would be better."

She nodded.

"I tried posting an ad for help at the feed store, but Joe wouldn't let me post it on the bulletin board because he said I couldn't prove I could pay for the work. Won't that be a problem?" she asked.

"Could be, but I think putting it in my name won't hold things up. We need to let people know things are different at the ranch. Build its reputation again."

"I don't want my dad to hear about this until he's stronger."

"Your call, but think about this. He's probably worrying himself sick knowing how things were when he had his stroke. Knowing you're there. Without knowing things have changed, he's going to continue to worry about stuff and that can't be good for recovery."

"What if he's angry I'm doing this?"

"You need to explain the buyback clause. I'm not taking over the whole ranch, it's a buy in partnership. I think he'll rest easier knowing things are changing."

"Maybe. I'll think about it."

When they finished eating, they finished the list of things they planned. The electric company said they'd try to get the power restored that afternoon. The same with the phone company.

"Buy enough food to feed you and me and two hands," he said when she dropped him at his truck. He was heading home while she grocery shopped before returning to the Bar-B-Bar.

"For how long?" She looked startled.

"We don't have time to run to town every couple of days. My mom usually buys for a month, then if we run short of one or two things, we usually have someone coming into town who can pick up some things. I'm heading for the feed store and then the newspaper. The sooner we get some help, the better for everyone."

Holly watched him get into his truck and drive away. She wanted to resent his confident attitude that by using his name he'd be able to get cowboys to work on the Bar-B-Bar, but she was grateful someone else was taking charge of things. What she knew about ranching wouldn't fill a single sheet of paper.

As she drove to the grocery store she wondered if it was Cody's plan to relegate her to the kitchen? Granted, someone needed to feed everyone on the ranch, but did it have to be her? She wanted to learn how to operate the place so she could be of real help, not stay in the kitchen all day feeding those working.

If she had a knack for it, she might consider staying even beyond when her dad needed her. So far, despite the lack of any amenities at the house, she wasn't having a horrible time. Must be the Braddock blood running through her veins.

She smiled when she thought how horrified her society loving mom would be if she had to spend a week without electricity or running water.

Or had to feed a bunch of cowboys.

Which raised the question–how to do that. How much food did four people eat–three of them working cowboys. Her mother cooked as little as possible. They ate out or ordered in more times than not. She could make breakfast, sandwiches. But the evening meal had to be pretty basic or they were all in trouble.

When she stopped at the store, she dug in her purse for some paper and tried to plan some basic meals she could fix, then calculate how much each man would eat. Knowing this was a first attempt, she was still surprised by the amount of food she'd need to buy. Good thing she had the pickup truck to take it all home. Now to see if she had enough money in her credit card to cover the cost.

When she filled one cart, she asked a clerk if she could park it in the front while she continued shopping.

"Are you Holly Braddock?" the woman asked.

"Yes."

"Cody Fallon told me you'd be in. I'll watch it for you and when you're ready, come to my line. I have the account number to put the bill on."

"I can charge it?"

The woman nodded with a smile.

They sure did things differently in Wyoming, Holly thought as she continued to pile package after package of meat in her cart.

Holly was delighted to see the power was on when she reached home. The place was almost cool with the air conditioner working. She'd worried the frozen food and refrigerator items would be a problem. Both units were working and cold when she opened them. She'd cleaned out the freezer and refrigerator earlier with all the spoiled food. Now they sparkled as she filled them quickly with the food she'd bought.

She tried the water and it came out of the spigot with force. No generator needed.

She put everything away, went to change into jeans and boots. It was delight inside the house, but she had to see if there was anything to do outside.

The heat was bearable as she walked to the barn. The

horses drifted to the corral fence to greet her. She stopped to pat each of them as they hung their heads over the top rail. She should have brought a treat. She'd seen Cody giving them apples and carrots.

She began to fill the water tank. When Cody's mare tried to stick her head in the hose while she was filling the tank, she turned the spray on the horse. Holly almost laughed at how much Starlight loved the water. The horse turned after a minute to get wet on the other side.

"Just don't roll in the dirt now," Holly told her finally putting the water in the tank. "You'll be covered with mud and I don't want to have to brush that all out."

She had no doubt Cody would expect her to keep his horse clean.

Coiling the hose away from the corral, she then went into the barn. It was dusty and getting hot. She looked overhead at the hay storage. Not much there. Sighing, she wondered how they'd get the place back in shape.

Holly heard a vehicle and went to the door. It was Cody's truck. He climbed out and she saw he'd changed, too. He was ready for work.

He looked up at the sky, then the horses.

"Let's take a ride, check on the perimeter fencing on the western side. I'm concerned after that breach on our property line that there may be other broken sections. I'd like a quick and dirty tally of the cattle, too."

"I just sprayed Starlight with water. She's all wet."

He gave her a grin.

"Yeah, she loves that. Sometimes when I ride her to the river, she wades in. I think she was a fish in another life. We won't be doing much but riding so let's try one of your dad's horses."

He quickly saddled both horses and watched as Holly figured out how to mount without his help using the wobbly corral fence. She was proud to find a way so she wasn't dependent on his help in everything.

"First thing tomorrow, we fix that fence," Cody said.

Holly watched as he quickly mounted, making it seem effortless. She wanted to be that capable.

As they headed out, Cody paid attention to the horse he was riding.

"Do you know their names?"

She shook her head. "I should have asked my dad. I will next visit."

Cody tried different maneuvers with the horse, all executed flawlessly.

"Good training. Now try yours," he said.

She tried to mimic his actions. The horse seemed to know more than she did. When she pulled to a stop next to Cody she was grinning. Even she knew the horse was good.

"Nice. I posted the jobs at the feed store, talked to a couple of ranchers while I was there. Walt Nelson said he could spare a man for a week. I took him up on it. The guy will be here early in the morning."

As they rode out Holly tried to imprint every detail on her mind. She wanted to be able to find her way around no matter what portion of the land she was on.

"Turn around and look behind you," Cody said at one point.

She complied and then looked at him with a question.

"Why?"

"That's the view coming back. If you only look ahead, you won't get the full picture. Sometimes things look differently coming from the opposite direction."

She nodded. It made sense. Every so often she'd look behind her, memorizing the contours of the hills or the spacing of the trees.

They crested a slight rise and before them was the main herd. There were cattle grazing as far as she could see. Some lying down, others cropping the grass.

Cody stopped and studied the herd.

Holly looked at the cattle and then at Cody.

"What now?"

"I'm trying to get an estimate of how many head's there. Have you looked at your father's records?"

"If you mean the ledger books in the office, I have, but I don't have a clue what they mean. Should I be looking for some kind of census of the cattle?"

He grinned. "Tally. There should be some information on the herd, number, ages, bloodlines, different things. Isn't he computerized?"

"There's a computer on the desk. We used to email," she said slowly. "Not as much as I should have."

"Maybe his records are on that."

"I'll have to check it. It's an old set up. I have a new laptop at home. If I can get my mom to send it to me, I'd rather use that."

"We'll get a new computer for the ranch. Set up the books to suit our new partnership."

She nodded already making plans to search through the

office that evening to find all she could about the business aspect of the ranch.

They rode until the sun was starting to slip toward the west and Holly was growing hotter each passing minute. Thankful for the hat and long sleeves, she still wished she could enjoy the air conditioning of the ranch house.

"This section of fencing looks good and tight. No breaches here. Your dad runs a good spread. I think things just got out of hand lately," Cody said

"Let's be honest, he beggared the ranch to send me to Europe for a year. Instead of telling me I was on my own, he spent money he couldn't afford. For a smart man, that was dumb," she grumbled.

Guilt mixed with anger. She shouldn't be angry with her dad, he wanted the best for her. But she couldn't help feeling irritated that he'd risked the ranch to indulge her. She would have lived a perfectly wonderful life never visiting Europe. Or taking a short vacation at some of the capitals. He hadn't needed to splurge so much.

Though she knew it was probably more complicated than that—and tied to his relationship with her mother.

"Sometimes I wonder how my dad and mom ever hooked up. They are so different and want such different things."

Cody nodded. "There's a lot to be said for like drawing to like. A city girl wouldn't be much use on a ranch. And if she wanted a night life, there's little of that most of the year."

Holly wondered if he was giving her an underlying message. She already knew he didn't expect her to stay. Nothing would convince him except still being here in the weeks and months ahead.

When they came upon a water trough filled by a windmill, the horses drank their fill. Holly knew she'd be achy from all the riding by the time she reached home, but for now it felt good to keep up with Cody.

"So did you always want to be a cowboy?" she asked.

"Guess so. Don't know anything else. We've had chores since we could walk. Learned to ride before I started school."

"It's a hard life," she said slowly, remembering he'd told her that more than once.

"Not so bad. Sometimes dealing with what Mother Nature tosses your way can get hairy, but mostly it's a good clean life."

She looked at her hands, dusty and grimy from their ride.

"Not so clean," she murmured.

He laughed.

"Not that kind of clean. The kind that keeps your soul intact. It can be hard work, but at the end of the day, you know you've done something."

"Did you pick up things from your father and grandfather or go to school?"

"We all went to college. I studied agriculture and business. Jarred studied the same thing. Kyle had EMT training and Tyler's our playboy But he still graduated from UW."

"I haven't meet Tyler."

"He's on the rodeo circuit. He's the baby of the group, spoiled rotten by mom."

She looked to see if he was serious, but the grin he gave her showed he was teasing.

"Do you all plan to work on the ranch forever?"

"Not me, I'm going to own part of the Bar-B-Bar. Maybe when your father retires, I can buy out his half and own it all."

"What about me?" she asked involuntarily.

"What about you?"

"I have some say. For now I am the other half of the ranch."

Cody gave her that slow smile that rocked her world.

"Yeah, but once your father's back in fighting shape, you'll head out, a job well done."

"That's what you keep saying. What if I decide I like this life? What if I want to make the ranch a success as much as my dad does? What if I never leave?"

He considered that for a long moment. Her expression was so sincere. He wanted to believe her. To think they could run the ranch together for all the years ahead.

But he remembered Jarred and Sheila. Heck even Frank and Holly's mom. Women not born to a ranching life rarely stayed.

He looked away, not wanting to fantasize about her staying. It was better that way. No sense in getting involved romantically with a temporary resident.

"Well?" she asked when he didn't respond.

"We can cross that bridge when we get to it," he replied.

Cody spent the rest of the afternoon going over different aspects of ranching. Almost like a lecturer, Holly thought. She tried to absorb all he was sharing, but as the afternoon waned, she paid less and less attention.

Her body ached. She was so hot she could fall face down in a puddle of water if it would cool her off. She had been given so many facts and figures her mind was spinning.

Was it his intent to have her absorb a year's work of training in an afternoon or was he trying to run her off by overwhelming her with all the aspects of ranching? He'd had decades to learn all this, she couldn't do it all in a day.

"Stop," she said, pulling her horse to stop.

He pulled back on the reins and looked over his shoulder at her.

"Problem?"

"No problem, I've had enough for one day and am heading for home. My brain is on overload. You can continue to ride around the perimeter or come back to the house, I don't care. But if you ride with me, don't talk."

Cody frowned.

"What do you mean don't talk?"

"I've heard enough. My brains are about to bleed out of my ears and I can't remember all you told me. I literally cannot stuff another fact into my brain today. No more."

She urged her horse into a walk, heading her for the ranch house–at least in the direction she thought she wanted to go. She hoped all the studying the landscape paid off. She'd feel like a total idiot if she wasn't going home.

12

Cody sat and watched her ride away. He wondered if she would make it back to her home, but decided to let her try on her own. People didn't learn just from hearing things. They had to try as well. At least she started off in the right direction.

He guided his horse to another copse of trees and dismounted. He'd give her a half hour head start. If she got lost, he'd hope he could spot her.

"Too bad they don't have part of the river running through their land," he told his horse, loosening the cinch and letting the animal graze on some of the sparse growing grass in the shade.

"I'd love to cool off about now."

Instead, he'd return to the corral, take care of his horse and then head for home. He had chores there to complete. And he wasn't going to give Jarred any ammunition to say I told you so.

Holly was delighted when she spotted the roof of the barn in the distance. She'd done it–found her way home all on her own. She looked around but didn't see Cody. She'd been a bit annoyed when he hadn't come with her but a certain sense of pride rose. She could find her way around the ranch. An important milestone.

She unsaddled the horse, brushed it down and turned it into the corral making sure there was plenty of water in the trough.

Almost unable to walk across the ground to the house, she kept an eye out for Cody. She refused to let him know how out of shape she was. Once inside, she headed straight for the bedroom and bath. A hot shower would help immensely.

Feeling refreshed a half hour later, Holly poured herself a glass of tea and glanced outside. No sign of Cody. Had he continued riding along the fence? All the fencing they'd seen had been strong. The only breach she knew of was the one that started this whole thing, along the boundary of the Rocking F.

She headed for the office, much more aware of what she needed to look for after listening to Cody's explanations all afternoon.

It was almost an hour later before Holly looked up. Glancing at the clock, she noted time to feed the horses. All were in the corral, so Cody had returned. She hadn't even heard his truck leave.

The horses taken care of, she returned to the kitchen and made herself scrambled eggs and toast. She didn't know what she was going to do about feeding herself, Cody and the cowboy who was coming to help tomorrow. She was so tired she just wanted to climb into bed and sleep until morning.

Cleaning the kitchen she went back to the office. Indulgences were off the table until she felt up to speed on the entire situation.

She called the nursing home to check on her dad, happy to learn he'd had a good day with the physical therapist and had gone to bed some time before and was already asleep.

That was the best she could hope for at this time.

She turned to the computer and began reading again. Her father had a good set of books, once she found access to them. She read back to the previous year and the one before that. It helped her understand the cycle of ranching.

Cody was right, there was a lot to learn.

Holly made a big pot of coffee the next morning and was pouring her first cup when Cody roared into the yard. A minute behind him another pick up truck pulled up. She watched through the window as a cowboy climbed out and met Cody between the two trucks. The loaner cowboy. She hoped she could keep up with them today.

They didn't even glance toward the house, but began walking to the barn. Cody stopped near the fence and noticed the horses eating. He glanced at the house then.

"Didn't think I was up, did you," she murmured, taking delight in his surprise.

She swallowed the hot coffee, not planning to rush right out there, though she wanted to. She couldn't wait to see him, hear him, spend time with him, even if he spent every moment teaching her like she was a child.

Briefly she toyed with the idea of waiting until he knocked on the door, but she wasn't sure he would. He could just continue on with the work he planned and ignore her.

Finishing her coffee, she picked up her gloves and hat and headed outside.

She heard them talking in the barn when she entered, letting her eyes adjust to the dimmer light.

"Good morning," Cody called. "Come meet Steve Canning. Steve, this is Frank's daughter Holly."

"Morning, ma'am," Steve said, touching the brim of his hat.

He looked to be about ten years older than Cody, his face bronzed by the sun.

"Good morning and thank you for coming to help us," she said with a warm smile.

She knew they were paying the man, but good manners never hurt.

"Glad to help," he said.

He looked at Cody. "Tools?"

"In here."

Cody led the way into the tack room and to the deep cupboard at the back. Holly watched, regretting she hadn't explored more of the barn so she'd known where the tools were.

In no time the men were digging new holes in preparation of new uprights to secure the cross polls of the corral. Holly watched for a while, taking in all Cody had done in preparation, from bringing new wood for the fence, to new hardware for a gate.

"What can I do?" she asked at one point.

"Wouldn't mind some water," Steve said.

"I have coffee made fresh just a little while go, any takers?"

They both agreed and both took it black.

She came back with two large mugs filled with the hot

brew. Cody took his, his fingers brushing against hers momentarily. She caught her breath and quickly masked it with a smile as she handed Steve his mug. Her heart raced at his touch.

"If you don't need me here, I'll be in the office. I'm making headway through my dad's records."

She thought she better put some distance between them. There was work to be done, no time for any daydreaming.

"It'll take most of the day here," Cody said, resting his cup on the edge of the sawhorse they were using to cut the poles to the desired length. He reached for another pole and laid it out, pulling out the tape measure.

"I could help here," she said.

He looked at her.

"Doing what? Have you built a corral fence before? Or any fence for that matter?"

She shook her head.

Cody put the pencil down and walked over to her, taking her arm and urging her toward the house.

"A partnership means many things. Among those are different skill sets the partners bring. I know my way around a spreadsheet, but it's not my most favorite part of ranching. You had training in that, maybe that would be your niche. Let us build the fence, you try to calculate exactly where the Bar-B-Bar stands financially which will give us a better understanding of what's needed from an investment aspect on my part."

"Okay," she said, wishing he'd ask her to stay to help in building the corral fence, but knowing what he said made sense. They needed a good estimate of what was required to bring the ranch back.

She hoped it wouldn't be more than he was willing to invest.

"I'll make lunch around one," she said when they reached the back porch.

"Sounds like a plan."

He turned and headed back to the barn.

"Sure, I'll sit at a desk all day and then work in the kitchen. Sounds just like what I've always dreamed of doing," she grumbled as she headed for the office.

Secretly she was pleased she wouldn't be spending the entire day on the back of a horse.

Once involved in the books, however, Holly began to appreciate Cody's plan. She was good at this and by the end of the morning had a good grasp of exactly how much money was owed and the status of the herd.

Holly didn't expect Cody on Saturday. He'd told her he was taking the day off and that he'd pick her up at six thirty for the dance at the Grange. She was glad for a day of rest. Between office work and doing new tasks that Cody thought she could handle, she had not visited her father except one evening after Cody left.

While sleeping in was not a luxury she could enjoy any time soon, she did plan a lavish breakfast at Rosie's after she fed the horses. A meal she didn't cook sounded the perfect way to have a day off.

Carrie Sue was behind the counter when Holly entered. She went to the empty seat at the counter and smiled at the waitress.

"Coffee?" Carrie Sue asked coming over to her.

"Please and the big breakfast. I'm splurging."

Carrie Sue smiled. "What's the occasion?"

"Not riding a horse today, not being lectured by a cowboy on every minute detail of ranch life, and the prospects of a dance tonight," Holly said, touching a finger with each item.

"Sounds like a great reason to splurge."

Carrie Sue took her order and then gave it to the cook. Checking on the other customers, she returned to Holly.

"So Cody's taking you to the dance tonight?" she asked casually.

"Yes."

"He's only ever taken one other woman to a dance. It caused a lot of gossip and he dropped her like a hot potato."

"We aren't involved except on a business level," Holly said softly.

She was uncomfortable talking about that in such a public place. She didn't want word to get back to her father about the partnership until after she'd talked with him.

"Ummm, maybe." Carrie Sue smiled again. "We'll see tonight, I reckon."

"You're going of course."

"Yes, I'm helping with the refreshments."

"No date?"

Carrie Sue glanced at the postcards on display on the wall near the cash register.

"I'm involved with a guy who travels all the time. Doesn't seem right to go out with anyone else. One day we're getting married."

"I didn't know you were engaged," Holly said.

"Not officially. But we've planned it for ages."

"Where is he now?"

"Who knows? Maybe in Nepal or Syria. It's a great job except it puts him in danger all the time."

"So when's the wedding?"

"When things settle down and he gets state-side assignments."

Holly took another sip of coffee, wondering when a foreign correspondent would ever want a state-side desk job. Sounded like Carrie Sue was in for a very long wait. Not that it was her business, but she liked Carrie Sue and it sounded as if she was getting the short end of the stick.

"How's your father?" Carrie Sue asked.

"Not recovering as quickly as I thought he would, but doing okay according to his doctor. It's going to be a long convalescence."

She refused to give voice to the prognosis the doctor made that her dad might never be fully recover. Miracles still happened. She was counting on it.

Carrie Sue chatted intermittently with Holly between serving other customers.

At one point Holly asked about what to wear to the dance.

"I didn't bring a lot of clothes. I never thought I'd be going to a dance while visiting my sick father. But then I didn't realize I'd be here this long."

"Most of us wear jeans and boots. The cowboys are wearing their best boots and hats, but just regular clothes. At Christmas we dress up fancy."

"Should I plan to bring anything?" Holly asked as she was finishing her meal.

"Naw, we cater it, so I'll be helping with that. My grandfather loves these kind of events. You'll get to meet him then. Enjoy your day."

She went to greet some new customers and Holly left money for the meal and went to the nursing home.

That evening butterflies danced in her stomach as she dressed for the dance. It seemed very casual to wear jeans to a party, but she did—wanting to fit in. It was awkward enough to be the outsider in a ranching community where everyone knew everyone else and everything there was to ranching.

She couldn't expect Cody to spend the entire evening with her, so she was psyched up to meet as many neighbors as she could and hope she clicked with one or two. Time to make new friends.

When Cody's truck pulled into the yard, she was ready. He'd obviously washed it as it sparkled in the sunshine. He got out—dressed like always, except every item from his hat to boots looked spanking new. She was glad she'd worn her new shirt with clean jeans and polished her boots. Her hair was loose, brushing her shoulders in a way that made her feel feminine, especially after wearing it in a pony tail all week to keep it out of the way.

"Ready?" Cody asked as she stepped out on the porch. "I guess so, you look mighty fine."

She felt a flush of pleasure at his compliment.

"So do you. I guess this was a good idea, I told my dad about it today and he seemed happy to hear I was going."

"Frank and my folks usually attend these. Most of the ranchers and cowboys in the area go. It'll be fun."

"Are your brothers going?"

"Heck, almost everyone from the Rocking F will be there. Carlos is staying at the homestead. The hands rotate who attend these things. Though Carlos never misses the Christmas dance."

The butterflies increased as they pulled into an already crowded parking lot.

Cody escorted her into the large hall. Chairs were placed along one wall. A band was tuning up in the back. The wall along the left contained two bars and long tables loaded with food.

Holly swore Cody knew everybody in the county and introduced her to every one of them.

When the band began to play, couples quickly moved to the center of the hall for dancing. Cody pulled her into his arms and began to twirl her around the dance floor in the Texas Two Step. Holly threw herself into the dance, feeling carefree and happy dancing with one of the best looking cowboys in the place.

When the song ended Cody gave her a hug and grinned down at her when he let her go.

"Fun, huh?"

"Yes. The most fun in a long while."

Before she could say another word, another cowboy tapped Cody on the shoulder. "Care to introduce the lady?" he asked.

"Nope," Cody said.

Holly smiled at the other man.

"I'm Holly Braddock. Frank Braddock's daughter."

"John-Paul Harrison, glad to meet you."

"Okay, so you met her, they're starting another song," Cody said, holding out his hand to Holly.

"Maybe the lady would like a different partner for the next one," John-Paul said, holding out his own hand.

Holly smiled at both.

"Actually, I'm still warm from the last dance. I think I's prefer something to drink."

Cody nodded and took her hand, throwing John-Paul a triumphant look.

"Come with me and I'll get us something."

"See you in a bit," John-Paul said, grinning at Cody.

"He seems nice," Holly murmured as they walked to one of the bars.

The music started again. Cody threaded his fingers through hers.

"JP's okay."

"But not to dance with?" she asked, teasing him.

He looked at her and shook his head.

"I thought we could dance again."

She nodded, looking around at the crowded room, the dancers again in full swing. She could dance the entire evening with Cody and be content. More than content. She'd love every moment.

He got them each a soft drink and they stood on the outskirts of the dance floor and watched the others. An older couple joined them.

"Thomas," Cody greeted the older man. "Katherine."

"Cody."

"I'd like you to meet Holly Braddock, Frank's daughter. Thomas and Katherine Bergon. They live outside of town in the opposite direction from the Bar-B-Bar. But I reckon Thomas has known your father all his life."

"Pert near. We were in grade school together. How's he doing? I was there last week. Tell you what, it's a sorry sight when a man my own age is laid low."

"He's gradually recovering," Holly said. "I'd love to hear some stories about when the two of you were young."

"Then come to dinner next week," Katherine said with a warm smile. "Thomas' mom was a great one for family pictures and I bet there are a bunch with your father as a little boy. To hear them tell things, the two of them practically lived at each other's house."

"Frank's a good friend," Thomas said.

He seconded his wife's invitation. Then looked at Cody.

"Want to come so she'll know the way?"

"I appreciate the invitation. What day?"

"Thursday?" Katherine said. "I'll make lasagna and that coconut cake you like so much, Cody."

"Sounds a treat. Can't wait."

He looked at Holly.

"Katherine's won ribbons at the county fair with her coconut cake. You'll love it," he said with a smile.

"I look forward to the evening," she said with a bright smile.

"How're you doing on the ranch?" Thomas asked. "Need any help?"

Holly shook her head.

"Thanks, but with Cody and Steve helping out, things

seem to be going fine. We're just holding things together until my dad gets better."

"You call on me if you need any help. I'll stop in and see your dad again this week."

The band started a slow song.

"This one's ours," Cody said, taking the soda can from Holly's hand and setting it down with his. He nodded to the Bergons and walked her out to the dance floor. Cody drew her into his arms, holding her pressed against him as they swayed to the slow song.

Holly's heart rate sped up being held so close. She relaxed and let the rhythm of the music dictate how she moved. Closing her eyes to savor the sensations racing through her, she gave herself up to the song and the delight of being in Cody's arms.

Slowly they danced around the room, moving in time to the beat, listening to the words sing about lost love and sad futures. She hoped she never experienced the lament of the song. She was too happy tonight.

When the music stopped, she slowly opened her eyes and gazed right back into Cody's amazing blue eyes.

He continued to hold her, staring back at her.

"That was nice," Holly said, not knowing what else to say. Not wanting to break the spell.

"You're nice," Cody said softly, and lowered his head to brush his lips across her.

Holly tightened her arms around his neck slightly, pressing against the hard body that still held her closely.

"Hey, bro, remember where you are?" Jarred bumped into them and looked at Cody.

Cody's arms dropped and he half turned to his brother. "Mind your own business, Jarred."

Jarred nodded and gave Holly an unfriendly look before sauntering away.

Holly looked after him, then back at Cody.

"He doesn't like me, does he?"

"He doesn't know you. Come on, let's get something to eat. It's hot in here. We can take it outside."

Holly was glad for the respite. She glanced around and noted to her dismay that others were staring at her. Did others in town view her presence with similar dislike?

Cody led them to the buffet tables, at the end of a small line.

Holly said hello to Carrie Sue who was standing near the first table.

"Hey, girl, having fun?" Carrie Sue asked.

Holly nodded and took the plate Carrie Sue offered.

"Help yourself. We sure don't want to take this food back to the restaurant," Carrie Sue said. "Though I don't have to tell Cody twice, right cowboy?"

"Hey, if y'all would stop making such good food, I could pass it by," he said, heaping his plate as he walked down the line."

"And if we did that, no one would come to the café and we'd be shut down in a New York minute," she retorted.

She winked at Holly and leaned closer, speaking in a softer tone. "Catch me later. I want to hear all about that kiss."

Holly looked at her in startled surprise. How could she not think the entire group had witness that kiss. She felt heat rise in her face. Embarrassment flooded. She nodded, vowing to leave as soon as possible. Glancing around, she didn't see anyone staring at her any more, but how many had seen Cody Fallon kiss her at the end of the dance?

What would have happened if his brother hadn't interrupted them?

She wished she knew. Safety lay in remaining partners in the ranch, nothing more. But her body argued the point. She wouldn't mind another kiss or two. Or even more.

To her surprise, Holly saw round tables with folding chairs scattered on the side yard of the Grange hall. The outdoor space was well lit with hanging lights. Most of the tables were already occupied. Cody headed for an empty one on the edge and put down his plate, turning to hold a chair for her.

"This suit you?" he asked as he sat across from her.

"Yes. It's fine."

She didn't look at him, but focused on the assortment of finger foods on her plate. Taking a piece of barbecue chicken, she took a bite.

"Wow, this is hot!"

She wished she had something cold to quench the fire in her mouth.

"Buffalo wings. We like'em spicy here."

He took a bite of one and chewed with relish.

"A warning would have helped," she said, taking a smaller bite.

It was tasty, just hot enough to burn her tongue.

"Want another drink?" he asked.

"Yes please and some water. My mouth may burn for a week."

"Milk cuts the burn, not water. I'll be right back."

He rose and leaned close to her. "Save my place."

She smiled, her face mere inches from his. For a moment he didn't move, gazing into her eyes. Then he straightened up and headed back inside.

Holly nibbled on her food, watching the others in the grassy area. She could tell a lot of tables held good friends from the laughter and conversations. Here and there she spotted a couple more intent on themselves than anyone around them. She recognized Kristi Donovan. She was leaning close to a tall cowboy. And from the looks they shared, Holly knew they had something special.

She wondered what it would be like to have one man interested in only her. Not for a fun evening or even a brief affair. Someone who'd be interested in building a life together.

Like her father and mother? The thought came unbidden.

She wished she knew more why they hadn't made it. Had they really tried?

Or at the first glitch had they ended the relationship?

Knowing her mother, she suspected the latter. How had her father reacted to the divorce? By the time she spent summers with him, the divorce had been final for years. Each had moved on.

Yet neither had ever married again.

That was interesting.

"Where's Cody?" Jarred Fallon stopped by the table and looked around.

"He went in to get us something to drink," she said.

Jarred pulled out a chair and sat down.

"How's your father doing?"

"Recovering."

Why had he sat down? She wished he'd leave and Cody would come back.

"This partnership thing is for the birds. Either your father will recover fully and want to take back the reins of the ranch or he won't be capable of doing so and will need to either get an excellent manager or see about selling the place. He's not going to want to be partners with anyone."

"You don't know that," she protested.

She was already concerned he might not see the partnership as the best solution. She didn't need Jarred adding to her uncertainty.

"I know your father–probably better than you do. I know how ranchers think. And from where I sit, I see you as a woman out for her own selfish means and latching on to the first man who thinks helping you will make a difference. Tell me, how much ranching knowledge do you have?"

"Not a lot, but I'm a quick learner," she said, glancing toward the Grange Hall. Where was Cody?

He shook his head in disgust.

"How many years did you stay away? Did you know how much your father talked about you–but not how you were a part of his life, more like you were some movie star he was stuck on. Holly looked so pretty in her prom dress. Holly sent me a post card from London. Holly and her mother are skiing in Aspen. You didn't mind taking his money but couldn't be bothered with even a flying visit."

She didn't have a reply. Everything he said was true to her immense regret.

"That's my seat," Cody said returning to the table. He set the two cans of soda down and glared at his brother.

"Keep your opinions to yourself," he said.

Jarred rose and faced his brother.

"I'm trying to make you see what you're getting yourself into. She isn't worth it."

Holly felt sick. She knew Jarred didn't like her, but not that his anger was so intense. She was guilty of all he said. She'd go back and change the past years if she could.

"That's to be seen, but the ranch is worth it. Either Frank gets better or he doesn't, but I can still run the place and make it pay."

"Pay for her trips to Europe," Jarred said scathingly.

"Whatever. She's got power of attorney, she's in charge. What she does is really none of our business, is it?'

"Unless she bleeds the ranch dry and you lose your shirt."

"It's mine to lose," Cody said, his voice still easy. "Take off, Jarred. Three's a crowd."

Jarred glanced at Holly and shrugged.

"Some have to learn the hard way."

"Like you did?" Cody asked, his gaze nailing his brother.

"Exactly."

Jarred turned and walked away.

13

Holly couldn't speak. She was mortified. And had no way to mitigate the situation. She had taken the money. She hadn't visited in ages. She and her father had grown distant with the years of separation.

Now she was trying her best to make it up before it was too late.

"Ignore Jarred. He has baggage."

She reached for the soda and took a long sip.

"Bad as it is to listen to him, he's right. I didn't visit for years. Didn't have as much communications with my dad as I should have."

She looked at Cody.

"Tell me the truth, Cody. Do you think my dad believes I'm only here now because I want more from the ranch?"

"Nope. I believe he knows you're here because he needs you. Family rallies around when needed."

Cody took a drink and then picked up another Buffalo wing.

"Don't let Jarred plant seeds of doubt. As I said, he has baggage."

"Let me guess, some gold-digger who took him for a ride."

"Nailed it in one."

"He thinks I'm one, too."

Cody shrugged. "Are you?"

Holly shook her head, insulted Cody would ask.

"Then who cares what Jarred thinks?"

"He's your brother, don't you care?"

"Not particularly. He's not my keeper. I can manage my own life. I'm not as dumb as he thinks because I'm taking a different path than he thinks I should."

"I'm not here to bleed the ranch dry," she said forcefully.

"I know that. You don't have to explain anything to me. I've seen you almost every day for the last several weeks. You're working hard to learn. You pull your weight. You care about your father and it shows. You don't have to justify anything to me."

She traced a pattern in the condensation on the can.

"Does everyone in town see me as your brother does?"

"Now how would I ever know what everyone in town thinks?" he asked with a smile.

"So not everyone, most people?"

She looked at him.

Cody saw the hurt in her eyes and he cursed his brother's interference.

"No. Unless he's talked to someone and I doubt it as that's not Jarred's style. I doubt anyone knows anything beyond your dad had a stroke and you came."

She took a deep breath.

Cody felt sorry for her. She was trying. Yet for some it wasn't enough. She had a long way to go before she'd be any good as a rancher in Wildcat Creek, Wyoming. And he wasn't sure his long range view was much different from his brother's.

She wasn't born and raised in Wyoming. She'd spent a year in Europe, flitting from place to place. Graduated college, granted, but so far had no job he knew about. Was she here only temporarily?

Or would she stay, given enough incentive?

"Would you be upset if I asked you to take me home now?" she asked, still studying the food still on her plate.

"Heck, yes. The evening's young. Finish eating and we'll go get some dancing in. I'm looking for another slow song."

She met his gaze with that.

"Why did you kiss me?"

"I wanted to. I've wanted to since practically I met you."

"Oh."

Her gaze dropped back to her food.

He reached out and captured her hand, holding it firmly.

"Don't you want to keep dancing? Tomorrow it's back to the routine. Let's have fun tonight."

She nodded, pulling her hand away with the pretense of picking up one of the small sandwiches.

They finished eating in silence.

Cody wished Jarred had not shown up, and especially that he hadn't been so ruthless in his cynicism. What went on in the Braddock family was none of his business.

Cody tried to keep his own uncertainty at bay. She said she'd stay. He was counting on that.

When they returned to the hall, Cody only claimed one dance before John-Paul was back. This time Holly danced with him. And after that song, another cowboy asked her.

Cody wandered to the edge of the room, watching her have a good time with different cowboys. He wanted her all to himself. And yet, he knew enough not to get involved with her. She was too different, had led a different kind of life than he knew or wanted. What if she didn't stay?

Cody shook his head in disgust. He was following her with his eyes as if he was afraid she'd disappear. Looking around, he saw Carrie Sue by the food tables watching the dancers. Her foot was tapping to the rhythm of the song.

"Care to dance, Carrie Sue?" he asked a minute later.

She studied him a moment and then nodded.

"I guess you're safe," she said with a lilt.

"Safe? Do I even want to know what that means?' he said as they moved to the dance floor.

"I have this fear that if I spend time with someone, everyone in town will draw the wrong conclusion."

"And that would be?"

"That I wasn't being faithful to Phillip."

"No fear there, girl. You never waiver in your devotion. I hope he realizes what a lucky guy he is."

The dance was fast and fun and both were breathing hard at the end.

Carrie Sue smiled up at him.

"Thanks, Cody, that was the most fun I've had in a while."

"Because I'm safe," he said, still wondering what she meant by that.

"From your attention to Holly, and that kiss I might add, I figure your interests are definitely elsewhere."

"Hey, we're just partners."

"Oh, is that what it's called these days." She laughed. "Go for it, Cody. She's really nice and I think you have a shot."

Cody started to explain, then remembered Holly wanted to be the one to tell her father about the partnership.

So break his word to her or have some people get the wrong idea.

"It's not like that," he said. Though he couldn't get the idea out of his head.

"You keep telling yourself that. Thanks for the dance."

Carrie Sue returned to the food tables, talking to her grandfather who was consolidating food on fewer trays.

Cody saw a couple of other young women in a group near the edge. Probably they'd like to dance, too. But he wanted to dance with Holly, not anyone else. Spotting her starting the dance with John-Paul again, he'd had enough.

He wound his way through the crowd and tapped his friend on the shoulder.

"Oh, not you again," John-Paul said with a mock groan.

"Me and my turn."

Cody grinned at Holly. "Okay?"

"Okay. Thank you, John-Paul."

Cody moved them away from the other man as fast as he could.

Holly giggled.

"You are so obvious."

"Well, I wanted to dance with you and not have him cut in."

"I'm having a good time, despite the caustic comments of your brother. Thank you for bringing me."

"And we have the drive home and the good night kiss to get to," he said audaciously.

Holly looked away, her body already humming with anticipation. A good night kiss! Oh, wow. The dance floor kiss had been something. She couldn't wait for a full blown kiss goodnight.

"Hey, there's a friend I want you to meet," Cody said, looking at a group of people near some of the chairs.

He took her hand and they walked over.

"Hey, Cody," the tall cowboy said.

Standing next to him was a pretty woman and beside her was a large German Shepherd dog wearing a service vest.

"Tuck. I want you and Jenny to meet Holly Braddock, Frank's daughter. Holly, Tucker Mason and Jenny Schofield."

"Call me Tuck," the man said offering his hand.

Jenny smiled at her. "How's your father doing? We heard he had a stroke."

"Recovering according to the doctor, but not very fast," Holly said.

She didn't want to go into the details. She still had some hope her dad would defy the odds and completely recover.

The two men began talking about futures on beef prices.

Jenny shook her head. "Cowboys always talk about cattle it seems."

"Do you live on a ranch?"

"Sort of, I rent a cabin from Walt Nelson. It's technically on his ranch, but looks more like a forest retreat. Tons of trees around. I'm a nurse."

"Your dog is beautiful."

"Thanks. His name is Val. He's my service dog but I'm about to take him off duty so Tuck and I can dance. Val would stick with me if he thought he needed to and that could cause complications with us and others dancing."

Holly wanted to ask why she had a service dog, but didn't know if she should or not.

The band started another song and both men turned.

"Another?" Cody asked with a grin.

"You bet," she said. "Nice to meet you both."

"We'll see you around," Jenny said as she began unfastening the service vest from her dog.

The song had a fast beat and provided no time for talking. When it was finished, the band segued into a slow ballad.

Cody drew her close.

"Why does Jenny have a service dog?" she asked.

"She was in the Army, has PTSD now from time in the Middle East."

"Oh."

She looked over his shoulder at the woman snuggling up with Tuck.

"She and Tuck are a couple, I take it."

"Yeah, they're engaged. The wedding is close to Thanksgiving, I think."

"Is everyone in town a cowboy or connected to one?"

He laughed softly. "Seems like it, huh? Wildcat Creek doesn't have any industry or such. It's completely surrounded by ranches large and small, so everything is geared to that."

He rested his cheek against her forehead and they moved with the music.

Would he kiss her again, she wondered, feeling flustered and excited all at once thinking about the possibility.

She tried to gauge her reactions to the sexy cowboy. She'd had a couple of boyfriends in the past, and a wonderful two weeks being shown all around Rome with a very romantic Italian. But she'd never been drawn to any of them as she was to Cody.

Holly didn't want him to know she was definitely

interested in that goodnight kiss he promised. She was in a world of trouble if she thought there could be anything between the two of them. She had her father to focus on and Cody had a brother dead set against her. She wasn't going to come between members of a family.

It was late by the time Cody and Holly decided to leave. She'd done her fair share of dancing. More often than not with Cody. But there were a few others who caught her attention. She wished she felt the attraction toward them she did toward Cody.

Sometime between leaving the Grange Hall tonight and tomorrow, she needed to get her priorities straight. Focus first on encouraging her father to get well. Then on learning all she could about how to run a successful ranch.

The contract, once signed, would contain a buy back clause. She was counting on it.

"Did you enjoy yourself tonight?" Cody asked when the town was left behind.

Holly rested her head against the back of the seat. Her feet hurt and she was so tired she hoped she didn't fall asleep on the drive.

"I did, thanks for inviting me. I met lots of people. I hope I can keep them all straight. And I loved all the dancing."

"You'll see them again and again and soon have them all straight," he said.

He switched on the radio and soft country rock filled the cab.

Holly gazed at the dark sky dotted with a million stars clearly seen twinkling in the vast expanse. She didn't remember the last time she'd seen such a display.

The headlights cut a path on the road, but the view from the side windows showed only darkness. She knew homes and cattle and fences dotted the land, but there was only darkness as they sped through the night.

The dance was unlike anything she'd been to in California. Certainly different from the embassy party she'd gone to in Rome. Casual, fun, neighbors and friends sharing a night together with dancing and good food.

She smiled remembering some of the lines the cowboys had tried on her. It felt like being the bell of the ball. Glancing at Cody, she could see the outline of his profile in the dim dashboard light. He was the most handsome cowboy she danced with. Though his friend John-Paul was the funniest.

When Cody turned onto her drive, her heart began to race. Was he serious about giving her a good night kiss?

He stopped near the back door. She rubbed her damp palms on her jeans and tried to see him clearly in the dark.

Licking suddenly dry lips, she asked, "Did you want to come in for coffee or something?"

"Better not. Dawn comes early. I'll walk you to your door."

He left the headlights on to illuminate the yard. Next time she needed to remember to leave on a light. It was really dark where there were no street lights.

When they reached the back stoop, she turned.

"Thanks again for taking me."

"It was definitely my pleasure," he said, drawing her into his arms.

When his lips touched hers, she sighed softly and kissed him back. It was even better than at the dance. He pulled her into his arms, molding her body against his, her softness to his rugged hardness. His mouth worked wonders as she delighted in the sensations coursing through her at his caresses, his hands running up and down her back, holding her close.

She put her arms around him and hugged him tightly as his lips continued their exploration. When he pulled back slightly to trail kisses on her cheeks, her eye lids, back to her mouth, she sought his mouth again, relishing the heat that exploded in her, her awareness of him rocketing off the charts. She could fly with Cody forever.

He pulled back a little and rested his forehead on hers. Both were breathing hard.

"I have to go," he said softly, not relinquishing his hold at all.

"I know."

Because if he didn't go, and soon, she'd do something foolish like invite him to stay. Blood pounded through her veins. Desire spiked higher than she ever remembered. She wanted this cowboy. She knew a night of passion would be beyond anything she'd imagined.

Not that she was giving into such desire. They were on the way to becoming business partners. She needed his focus on building back the ranch, not an attraction that could end badly and jeopardize the entire deal.

Still she didn't move. They had to stop, but she wanted to savor being held in his arms a little longer. That surely couldn't hurt.

"So I'll see you in the morning," Cody said softly.

"Yes. I'll be up early. Is Steve coming, too?"

"He said he would. I've got to go."

But he didn't move.

"Yes."

She didn't move.

Slowly he kissed her again, sweet and chaste, then let her go. Without another word, he headed for the truck.

Holly watched him leave, staring down the drive long after the taillights had disappeared.

"I can't have fallen for a cowboy," she said aloud. Then laughed. "I think I have."

The next morning Holly rose early, still tired from a restless night. She'd spent far too much time reliving the dance, the final kiss at the door. The last thing she wanted Cody to know, however, was how much time she spent thinking about him.

So up early, a quick breakfast and then out to feed and water the horses.

When she leaned against the new rail fence a short time later, she noticed immediately how sturdy it was. Thanks to Cody. Once they had a plan in place, every aspect of the ranch would be brought back to tip top shape.

She hoped her father would be pleased.

Maybe she should tell him of the partnership before they signed the final papers.

On the other hand, she had no other choices and wouldn't renege on the agreement with Cody for anything. She was counting on her father to agree it was a good idea and that he could see the benefits of having a younger man in charge.

Of course Cody would only be in charge until her father bought out the one percent to make him the majority partner.

She knew next to nothing about running a ranch. She hoped she could learn fast enough to be a help.

The phone rang and Holly stopped musing and ran to get it. It could be Cody saying he was coming later.

"Hello?"

"Holly Braddock?"

"Yes." She didn't recognize the woman on the other end.

"This is Sunnyside Convalescent Hospital. Your father suffered another stroke a short time ago and was transported to the hospital in Coleville."

"What? Is he okay, will he be okay?" Fear rushed through her. He had to be okay. He had to be.

"I don't know. They will release that information to next of kin and that's you."

"I'll get to the hospital right away."

Fear knocked her for a loop. She thought he was recovering. Another stroke wasn't good.

She grabbed her purse and keys and ran for the truck. She prayed he'd be all right.

The traffic was nonexistent so early on a Sunday morning. Glad it was a straight drive to Coleville she pushed as fast as she dared.

She made record time driving to the hospital. Dashing into the emergency room, she went to the desk.

"Frank Braddock, he was brought in a short time ago with another stroke. I'm his daughter."

The nurse looked at her computer screen and nodded.

"He was taken right up to intensive care. His doctor was notified and arrived ten minutes after Frank."

She looked compassionately at Holly's frightened

expression. "They're doing all they can, hon. He's a tough ol' rancher. I hope he pulls through."

"Me, too," she said. "Which way to intensive care?"

She followed the directions praying all the way. When she reached the ICU, the nurse at the desk looked up.

"Can I help you?"

"Frank Braddock? I'm his daughter Holly."

"I don't have an update for you, Miss Braddock. He was transported by ambulance, seen in the emergency room and then transferred here. His doctor's in with him now. If you have a seat in the waiting room, I'll have him come see you as soon as he's free."

"Can I see my dad?"

"Not yet. Let's see what the doctor says first."

Holly went to the waiting area across from the desk. She was too antsy to sit, so paced the small area, keeping constant watch at the reception area to see the doctor as soon as he got there.

Her phone rang ten minutes later.

"Hello?"

"Where are you?" Cody asked.

"I'm at the hospital in Coleville, my dad had another stroke and they brought him in. Cody, I'm scared. What if he doesn't make it?"

"I'll be there as soon as I can make it," he said.

"You don't have to–" she started to say, but he had already disconnected.

Cody didn't need to come in. She started to call him back, but then stopped. She'd love to have someone there to lean on. She was so scared. What if her dad died? She hadn't told him how much she loved him. How much she regretted the time spent apart. Or that she wanted to be here for him as long as he needed her.

She gazed out the window at the early morning. The hospital grounds were lovely, with lush green grass, walkways winding through the lawns, and patches of colorful flowers growing here and there. She scarcely noticed.

Was she serious about staying?

Wyoming had always been a fun place to visit. If asked, she would have said she was a California girl. Something about this land drew her, however. Maybe it was knowing it was her father's legacy. His family—their family—had owned the land for one hundred years. She could visit the town cemetery and see the graves of those who had gone before, those who had built the ranch, enjoyed the community of Wildcat Creek for generations.

She wanted to be part of that.

Her mother would never understand.

And she wasn't one hundred percent sure she understood it herself, but as she waited for word on her father, she vowed to do whatever it took to build her life right here.

Easier said than done, but she was determined. Others might doubt, but the only convincing she could be sure of was to stick it out and be here in the months and years ahead.

She resumed pacing, checking her watch. It's been an hour since she got the call from Sunnyside. What was taking so long? Was her dad going to be okay?

Stress built. She considered going back to the desk to ask the nurse, but Holly knew she wouldn't have any more information than before.

Cody strode down the hall, cowboy hat on his head, boots sounded against the linoleum tiles.

She saw him and burst into tears.

"Hey, Holly, don't tell me he died," Cody said, reaching her and pulling her into his arms.

She shook her head.

"I don't know anything more than he had another stroke. No one has told me anything and I'm still waiting for his doctor."

She clung to him, glad for his strength, for his presence just being with her.

"They'll let you know as soon as they can," he said, rubbing her back.

She nodded, and pulled back.

"Sorry, I'm getting your shirt wet."

"There's tissue over there," he said, nodding toward a table at the side of the waiting area.

"They probably need it lots here," she said, walking over and snatching up a couple of tissues and blotting her eyes. "Thanks for coming. You didn't have to."

"Hey, partners stick together."

She nodded, trying to stop the tears.

"I'm so scared, Cody. What if he doesn't make it?"

"Don't borrow trouble from the future. We'll know more when you talk to the doctor. I see his not coming out as a good sign. He's still working on your dad. Don't you think?"

"Maybe. I just wish I knew more."

"Hold on and I'll see what I can find out," he said.

He went to the nurses' station. He recognized the nurse there. Beth had gone to high school with him.

"Hey, Beth," he said.

"Hey yourself, Cody. You here with Miss Braddock?"

"Yeah. Any word on her father?"

She shook her head.

"I told her the doctor would be out as soon as he knew something. The longer he's in there, though, the more likely it is the patient's still hanging on."

"I figured that much. I'm going to take her to the cafeteria for some coffee. Can you page us or something if the doctor comes out?"

"Give me your cell phone number and I'll call you."

Cody recited the number then went back to Holly.

"Come on, let's get some coffee. We could be here a while."

"You go. I'll wait here."

"No, you need to move around, not just worry about your dad. Come on. The nurse will call us if the doc comes out before we get back."

He could tell Holly didn't want to go, but reluctantly let him take her hand. She looked at the nurses' station once more then walked with Cody to the elevator.

The hospital wasn't large, only three stories tall. The cafeteria was on the ground floor. They were there in only seconds. There were few tables occupied. Walking to the food area, Cody asked her what she wanted.

"Just coffee."

"Did you have any breakfast?"

She nodded.

"Before the call. I fed the horses, too."

"Steve's there. I checked when I first got here. He'll stay all day and feed them before heading out tonight."

She nodded again.

He bought two coffees and handed her one.

"You take yours with cream, right?" he asked.

She nodded again.

"Holly?"

She looked at him. "What?"

"Do you want to pray for your dad?" he asked softly.

She nodded and they both bowed their heads.

"They're doing all they can for your dad," Cody said softly a minute later. "I know you're worried, but he survived the first stroke, he'll probably pull through this time, too."

"You don't know that for sure," she said.

"I don't. But either way, you need to stay on top of things. If he survives, he needs to get better. If he doesn't, you'll be in charge of the ranch and need to decide how things will go in the future."

"Well, that's blunt," she commented, walking over to the condiments stand and taking the top off her coffee to add cream. Once done, she took a sip.

"Honest," he said.

"I know. I just can't imagine a world without my dad. I want to make up the time we were apart. I want some more years to get to know him, learn how to run the ranch, see what I can do with my life."

"Here in Wyoming? If he dies, you'll be free to return to California."

She looked at him, frowning.

"Let me get this straight. You think I'm just here for my dad."

"Aren't you? You haven't visited for years. Granted, he

fell ill and you came right away. But once he's gone, there's nothing holding you to Wildcat Creek."

"You're wrong. And so's my mother. My family has owned the ranch for generations. It's not going out of the family on my watch."

"Fifty percent is."

"With a clause to buy back one percent, so it'll still be the family ranch. And who knows, maybe one day I'll have enough money to buy back that forty-nine percent."

"Yeah, maybe."

"You don't think I can do it, do you?"

He studied her for a long moment.

"Actually, I do believe you could do it. Whether you will or not remains to be seen."

"You sound like Jarred."

"Ouch. Not that."

She smiled.

"Okay, not that bad. I don't know how to prove myself except to stay long enough to show everyone."

"That's the spirit. Come on we'll go back up."

They went back to the waiting room and sat side by side.

Holly sipped her coffee, the worry fresh. When her phone rang, she answered it softly, knowing she wasn't supposed to be talking on the phone in the hospital.

"Wait, I have to go outside."

She looked at Cody.

"It's my mother. I'm going outside to talk to her. Come get me if anything changes."

He nodded.

"Where are you?" her mother asked when Holly spoke again into the phone.

There was a bench near the hospital's double doors and she sat down, glad for the warmth of the early morning sun.

"I'm at the hospital. Dad had another stroke. I'm waiting to hear how he's doing."

There was a long silence on the other end.

"I'm sorry to hear that," her mother said. "That doesn't sound very encouraging. What are you going to do if he's a vegetable or something?" her mother asked.

"Mom!"

"Face facts, Holly, multiple strokes don't sound like a full recovery is on the horizon. You need to understand the man you knew may be gone forever. He could even have another stoke and die."

"I know."

She took a deep breath. She prayed he wouldn't die, but knew that was a strong possibility. Regret and guilt ran deep. Was her prayer for his recovery only so she could make things up to him?

No, she wanted him to live, to recover and to resume the life he loved. Loved more than her mother or he would have given in and gone away to make a different life when her mother couldn't take living on the ranch.

"So what are you going to do?"

"I've told you before, I'm staying here. I really need the money my car would bring."

"I'm not letting you waste a dime on that ranch. Your father's always been land poor, lots of acres, not much money."

"If you knew that, why take the money he sent each month?"

"He owed me."

Holly took another breath. This argument was for another time. She wanted to get back upstairs.

"Why did you call?" she asked in a calm voice which belied the turmoil she felt inside.

"When are you coming home?"

"Mom! I just told you Dad had another stroke and you think I should be thinking of coming home? I'm staying. In fact, I'm staying forever if dad lets me."

"What? You can't stay there. I lived on that ranch for three years. It's bleak in winter, hot as Hades in summer. There's no social life and nothing to do. It's not like your father found oil on his land like the Fallon's. They make it all look so easy with money flowing like the oil they pump out. It's a hard life, Holly, not what you're used to at all."

"Oh," Holly said.

She hadn't known the Fallons had oil. No wonder Cody could afford to buy into the ranch. If his family was wealthy from oil, he could buy the entire ranch.

And it also explained Jarred's animosity. He probably thought she was after Cody's money. Which she didn't even know he had until right now.

"Oh, what?" her mom asked.

"Nothing. Actually, I need to go. I'll call you in a few days."

Before her mother could protest, Holly hit the off button and put her phone back in her pocket. She finished her coffee, tossed the cup in the nearby trash can and headed back to the ICU.

Cody met her when the elevator door opened.

"I was coming for you," he said. "The doctor's at the nurses' station and wants to talk to you."

"Could you tell if it was good news?"

"From that poker face, no."

Holly and Cody walked back to where the doctor was jotting notes on a clipboard.

He looked up and smiled at Holly.

"Frank's a tough old bird. This stroke was caught shortly after it happened. He's stable and doesn't appear to have suffered any additional damage. Still a bit early to tell, but I think he's about where he was yesterday in recovery from the first stroke. We'll keep him here for a day or two and make sure he doesn't have another one."

"What caused it, do you know?"

He shook his head.

"No more than the first one. We went over the possible causes before. His blood pressure is stable and well within normal range. He doesn't meet the other criteria, so it's just a stoke happening without a cause and effect."

"Would worry acerbate the situation?" she asked.

"It could," he said.

"Anything we can do?" Cody asked.

"No. You can visit him in a few minutes. He's awake and alert. Then he'll need rest."

Holly turned to Cody.

"I think we should tell him of the partnership. I was planning to talk to you about it today anyway. Maybe it will stop any worries about the state of the ranch."

"Fine by me," Cody said.

When they entered Frank's hospital room, Holly was glad

to see her dad awake and smiling at her. Granted the left side of his face was still slightly paralyzed so the smile was lopsided, but she was reassured he knew her and was glad to see her.

"Hi, Dad," she said, going to his side and giving him a kiss on the cheek. "You gave me another scare."

He nodded. "Sssoorrree."

"Just get better. Cody's with me. And we have something to tell you."

Frank looked from Holly to Cody.

"The thing is, Dad, I don't know much about ranching. But Cody does. He's been helping me out."

Frank nodded at Cody.

"The ranch needs help, you know."

Frank looked back at her, regret on his face.

"I don't know all the ins and outs, but it needs an influx of cash and someone who knows how to run it until you get back. That's not me. So–"

She hesitated, and looked at Cody.

"We propose a partnership, Frank. You and me. Fifty-fifty to start."

Frank stared at Cody. Tears filled his eyes.

"Oh, no, Dad, we don't have to do it. We haven't signed anything yet," Holly said distressed at the tears.

"Tttaank ooou," he muttered, still holding Cody's gaze. He nodded.

"Hey, that's what friends do. You know that. We'll have the place in great shape before long and you can rest easy and focus on getting well. When you're back on your feet, we can discuss things."

Cody was touched by the older man's gratitude. He knew it was a solid plan and was reassured that Frank saw that, too.

Slowly Frank raised his right hand and stretched it out toward Cody. The cowboy knew exactly what it meant as he grasped it for a firm handshake. It was how things were done in Wildcat Creek.

14

When they left the hospital, Cody suggested they get something to eat before returning to the ranch. Holly concurred and they arranged to meet at Rosie's. When they arrived, they settled in one of the booths, ordered and updated Carrie Sue on Frank's condition.

"I'm so relieved he went for the partnership," Holly said while they waited for their food.

"Did you think he wouldn't?" Cody asked.

"I wasn't sure. I believe it's the right thing to do. At least for the ranch. Is it the right thing for you?"

"Let me worry about me."

She studied him for a moment.

"I didn't know you had a lot of money."

He met her gaze. "Define a lot."

"More than me, that's for sure. And mom said the Fallons have oil on a their land, so you must be really wealthy."

"I think your mom's envious."

"Of course she is. She wants to be fabulously wealthy."

He smiled.

"We're ranchers, tied to the land, the cattle, and subject to the capriciousness of nature. Granted the oil adds a cushion in bad years. But we're still ranchers," he said.

"That's why Jarred's so against me, isn't it? He thinks I want to exploit you for your money."

Cody smiled again.

"Honey, you're way too transparent to be a gold digger. Jarred got burned once. I think he sees all women the same now. I know you're not a gold digger."

Holly was grateful he didn't see her that way. She wondered if Jarred would ever see her for who she was, a woman trying to hold on to her dad's place to pay back all he'd done for her.

"I'm so glad my dad's okay with the partnership," she said. She hadn't realized how much she was worried he wouldn't be until she felt the relief at his reaction.

"Yeah, he did seem happy about it," Cody said.

Carrie Sue brought their lunches, both chose hamburgers with everything and fries. The plates were heaping. For a moment Holly wondered if she could eat it all, but she was suddenly famished with the relief of her father's situation and dug in.

Her cell rang and she answered. A moment later she responded, "As it happens, we are in town right now. We could probably be there in about an hour."

She looked at Cody.

"It's the attorney. The agreement is ready, do you want to swing by and sign today?"

"We can pick up a copy and take it to read. Sign in day or two," Cody said.

Holly relayed that and then said they'd be there before long. When she set her phone down, she looked at Cody curiously. "Are you having second thoughts?"

"Nope."

"Then why not sign today?"

"I want to read through it, make sure it says what we want. And I don't want to be pressured when doing that. We can sit down together and read it through, if we agree, we sign. Then we plan."

"Plan what?"

"What we're doing first," Cody said, swiping a french fry into ketchup.

"We'll be able to make it a paying ranch again, won't we?" she asked.

"Trust me, Holly, we'll make it a strong, money-making enterprise."

She nodded. She did trust him. Without his help, she'd be forced to close down, sell cattle at a loss and who knows what that would do to her father. She wasn't sure why Cody was so supportive. But she was grateful.

She glanced at him as he ate. She felt warmth invade her. She could look at him all day. She'd never felt like this around another man. She had to hold on to any emotions. Could gratitude be confused with love?

Did he see her as anything but a neighbor to help?

Cody headed for the Bar-B-Bar after lunch while Holly went to the attorney's office. Once she received the agreement, and discussed the next steps with Nathan, she stopped by the grocery store to pick up a few things.

She wasn't the greatest cook in the county, but did her best to feed Cody and Steve hearty meals. She'd be back at the ranch by mid afternoon, enough time to get the financial reports printed so Cody would know the full extent of their situation.

As she drove along the familiar highway to the ranch, she felt a wave of gratitude rise for the neighbor who was willing to help her. She vowed to do all she could to make this relationship a success. And do it without complaining.

She blamed herself for her father's situation. He should never have continued to give her so much. Still, the past was past. Time to rectify things and make a brighter future.

Cody's truck was near the barn when she drove in. She didn't see him or Steve. Unloading the groceries, she made a stew, prepped for cornbread and then headed for the office.

The men came into the kitchen after six. Both looked tired and hot. Holly was glad for the air conditioning and she knew they had to be, too.

They each served themselves stew from the pot on the stove. Holly cut the cornbread and set it on the table. No one talked much as they began to eat.

Once everyone seemed to be slowing down, Holly asked how the day had gone.

Steve talked about working on some of the water holes, explaining how they could get choked with weeds if not kept clear. He said he had to get back to Walt's place after dinner, but would return in the morning.

"Thank you for helping out. I don't know what we'd do without you," Holly said with a smile. She glanced at Cody. "Though I'm sure Cody would have come up with some solution."

"Oh, some cowboy came by earlier today. Charlie Lambert. I gave Cody his phone number. He's hunting work," Steve said.

"We'll call him this evening," Cody said, taking another square of cornbread. "This is a great dinner. Thanks."

She smiled. She wasn't a especially adept in the kitchen so it was nice to hear the praise. She didn't mind cooking for now, but wanted to make sure she learned more about ranching than merely spending time in the kitchen.

She made short work of cleaning up when Steve left. She washed the dishes and put them on the drain rack.

Without being asked, Cody found a clean dish cloth and began drying the dishes and silverware.

"You don't have to do that," she murmured.

"Many hands make light work, as my Mama always says" he murmured. "Beside, I want to review the agreement as we planned and I'm tired. The sooner this is done, the sooner we can move on."

"I printed out all the reports that came up in my dad's program. I want you to look at them in case they tell you things I'm missing."

He nodded. "You'll be up to speed in no time," he said.

She hoped he was right.

They spread the reports out on the dining room table which had more room than the office desk. Cody read through them one at a time, explaining them to Holly as he went.

"So you can see how much potential this place has," he said laying down the last report.

"And I can see where Dad should have used money to repair things instead of spending on me," she added, staring at the report.

"Not your fault. He's an adult. If that's how he wanted to spend his money, who are we to say different? Beside, he didn't plan on having a stroke. Who knows what plans he did have to bring in some money?"

"Like what?"

"I don't know. I'm just saying we don't know everything."

He reached out and took her hand in his, squeezing gently.

"But we can decide how we'll handle things and let him know when things turn around," he said.

She met his eyes. "Do you really think we can pull this ranch back into the black?"

He nodded, his gaze steady on her.

Holly smiled. She trusted Cody.

"Then let's go over that agreement so we can start moving forward."

They read the agreement word for word. Once or twice Cody suggested slightly different wording. Holly was fine with the changes. When they finished, she placed it back in the envelope the attorney had given her.

"So tomorrow we can go to Nathan's and finalize."

"Maybe the next day. There was a breach in one of the cross fencing I wanted to get to tomorrow. I've called on one of our men to help. I thought Steve could show you how to clean out watering holes."

She would have rather gone with Cody, but nodded.

"Now, let's call this guy and see if we have a possible addition to the ranch," Cody said pulling the note from his pocket.

They went into the office to call the prospective employee. The phone didn't have a speaker feature, so Cody tilted the receiver so Holly could also listen.

After a minute, however, she found it more difficult to pay attention to the conversation than react to Cody's nearness. His warmth seemed to envelope her. His voice reverberated through her. She leaned against his strength and would have sworn she grew stronger.

He asked the man to come to the ranch by six and they could all have breakfast together.

When he hung up he pulled away and Holly felt cold. She shook off her mood and rose.

"So we might have a new cowboy. Do you think Walt will let Steve continue a little longer?"

"I expect so. I can get a couple of men from the Rocking F as well when we need them. It's getting late and I need to get home. We didn't get our list drawn did we? Tomorrow will have to do."

She nodded, wishing he could stay. Hoping the agreement would be signed and then maybe he'd want to stay on the Bar-B-Bar instead of going home to the Rocking F each night.

But where would he stay?

The next thing to deal with was the bunkhouse. She needed to make sure it was habitable for any cowboys who would be working on the ranch.

Cody rose and took her hand. "Walk me to the door."

"I just thought about the bunk house. I'll need to make sure it's ready for Charlie Lambert to stay in if we hire him. He sounded good on the phone."

"He did. We'll check him out tomorrow. If he stays after breakfast to help out, that'll give you a chance to call his references."

He picked up his cowboy hat in the kitchen and headed for the door.

"Goodnight, Holly," he said, lowering his head to kiss her goodnight as if it was the most natural ending to the evening.

Holly watched from the doorway until the taillights of his truck were no longer visible. She wished he had stayed. She wished he'd kissed her more than once.

Cody drove down the dark driveway wishing he didn't have to leave. It would have suited him to a T to climb the stairs to the second floor and stay the night. To stay every night.

Whoa, where had that thought come from? He hardly knew Holly. Though he was drawn to her as he'd never been to any one before.

Yet there was always the possibility she wouldn't stay. Jarred sure thought she wouldn't. If the ranch was back in the black, would she stay or would she flit off again, seeing the world, spending her father's money?

That wasn't fair. Hadn't she said she hadn't known he was practically bankrupting the ranch to fund her trip to Europe?

Instead, he visualized them working together in the future, repairing what needed repairing. Expanding the herd. Giving the place a face lift once they were operating in the black. Expanding when they could. Riding out together.

He still hadn't taken her to the swimming hole. Maybe they could do that if they hired Charlie and Steve stayed on a bit longer. They could easily refurbish that gate between the two ranches. He'd have to let Jarred know if he planned to go swimming so the men would know to stay away or at least bring swimming trunks. A nice picnic under the trees near the water would be in order when they wanted to rest.

He was jumping the gun.

But he couldn't help thinking of what could be.

When he reached the Rocking F, he bypassed the main house and drove to his own smaller place. He hadn't told Holly how much money he had, but his share of the oil proceeds, plus the salary his father paid, would enable him to buy the Bar-B-Bar lock, stock and barrel. He hadn't used any of the money over the years and had no problem planning to use a portion to bring the ranch back. It'd go a long way to easing Frank's mind, too.

Charlie Lambert showed up at the appointed time the next morning and joined Steve, Cody and Holly for breakfast. He was tall and lanky and looked to be pushing forty. But there was no doubt he was a cowboy through and through by the way he dressed, walked and talked.

In no time the three men were talking cattle and hay prices and branding practices. Holly soaked up every word. She could learn a lot from these men who had been working on ranches for years, if not their entire lives.

She liked Charlie and tried to get a read from Cody what he thought of the cowboy. His demeanor gave nothing away.

When they finished eating, Cody invited Charlie to ride with him for the day.

"Didn't bring my horse. Wasn't sure if I'd be staying," Charlie said.

"You own your own horse?" Steve asked.

"Yep, really great cow pony. He's savvy like you wouldn't believe."

"Always nice to have a horse like that," Cody said. "We have some horses who are still getting over being neglected for a while, but they'll hold up for the day. Holly will call the references."

Charlie nodded and pulled out a folded paper from his back pocket and handed it to Holly.

"Thanks for a mighty fine breakfast, ma'am," he said.

Holly smiled. "My pleasure."

She was glad she could manage eggs, pancakes and sausage.

Steve and Cody also thanked her for the meal and she smiled, amused to see them follow Charlie's lead. Neither had thanked her for breakfast before.

Not that she needed that. She was learning as she went and wanted nothing more than to pull her weight on the ranch.

She had prepared sandwiches and cookies for each of the men as she didn't expect them back for lunch. That gave her the entire day to do things around the homestead.

After dishes were done, and it was a reasonable hour, Holly called the two references Charlie had given.

Both had high praise for the cowboy. He'd worked several years for the first ranch, down in Colorado, and the rancher had only good things to say about his work and loyalty. He'd been at the ranch in Utah for only a few years, but again the rancher had nothing but good to say. When asked why he left, they both said he was trying different locations to see if he'd like to settle down. One thing was he'd never let her down while he was working for her and give her plenty of notice if he wanted to move on.

Satisfied with what she heard, she hoped Cody liked him enough to hire him. And if that was the case, the bunkhouse needed work immediately.

She spent the rest of the morning giving the common area of the bunk house a thorough cleaning, and then moved into one bedroom and then a second one. There were ten all told, but unless Steve wanted to stay over she only needed one for Charlie and one for Cody if he decided against going back to the Rocking F each night.

Another day she'd finish with the other bedrooms.

Holly had dinner almost ready when the men rode into the yard.

She planned steak, potatoes and corn on the cob, all she could cook on the barbecue she'd found on the back of the house. It had an almost full propane tank, so she planned to use it often.

While she was keeping an eye on the steaks, Cody joined her.

"Did you call Charlie's references?" he asked.

"Yes. There were only two, but cover the last twelve years. Both men spoke highly of him and both said they'd hire him back when I asked."

"He's knowledgeable and had a couple of good ideas today when we were going over things. I'm comfortable hiring him if you are," he said.

She nodded, pleased that Cody wanted her agreement.

"I like him," she said. "I cleaned up the bunk house today, the living area and two bedrooms. I didn't know if you or Steve might wish to stay here overnight instead of leaving each evening."

"I'll check with him. Good idea."

He looked as if he wanted to say something and Holly waited. But he watched the steaks sizzle and didn't say anything.

Dinner was almost finished when the phone rang. Holly answered it and then looked at Cody.

"It's for you," she said, holding out the receiver.

He took the phone. "Fallon."

To his surprise it was Ed Stinner.

"I heard you're running the Bar-B-Bar now," Ed said. "I'd like to have my old job back. I know that ranch like the back of my hand and would like to be back there."

His voice sounded hesitant.

Cody's initial reaction was to tell him no way. But from a business point of view it wouldn't hurt to have a man working who knew the ranch.

"From the word I hear around town, you weren't happy at all when you left."

"Yeah, sorry about that. I was mad I didn't get paid. But when I hear you're running the place, I knew that would never be a problem again. Fallons practically own the area. Your reputation is top notch. I'd appreciate being given a second chance."

"I'll get back to you," Cody said. "What's a good number?"

He jotted it down on a pad near the phone then hung up.

Everyone looked at him.

"Ed Stinner wants to come back to work here," he said, his eyes on Holly. "Something we can discuss after dinner."

"Isn't he the one badmouthing my dad?" she asked recognizing the name.

Cody nodded.

"We'll talk later."

The cupcakes for dessert were a hit. Each man took three and all thanked Holly for the treat.

She was glad she'd thought of them.

Steve left and Cody and Charlie went into the office. Holly decided she didn't need to be there when he was offered the job. He'd report to Cody, not her.

"He accepted the job," Cody said coming into the kitchen just as Holly dried the last dish.

"He's staying the night and tomorrow will go get his horse and his things."

"Good."

"It's cooled down a tad and if a breeze comes up, it'll be nice to sit outside for a while."

"You've been outside all day," she said, already heading for the door.

"Enjoy it while we can. Winters are too cold to sit outside."

Once they were seated on the porch, Cody said "I talked to Steve today and offered him a job. But he's been working for Walt for a number of years and has a good relationship with him and the others on the ranch and wants to go back."

"So what do you think about Ed?" she asked.

She'd never met the man, but she didn't like knowing he'd been complaining about her father. Or the fact he'd just walked off the ranch.

Cody rocked back in the chair he was in.

"Not sure. He's a good worker I've heard. I'm pretty sure your father liked him. Some folks live paycheck to paycheck and it's a real hardship when the money stops coming in."

"How many cowboys do you think it'll take to run this place?" she asked, gazing over the landscape, feeling the warmth of the evening seep into her.

"Probably three or four plus you and me," he said.

She loved this portion of Wyoming. She'd loved visiting when she was a child, and she felt the call of the land now. She'd made up her mind to stay. Every day seemed to strengthen her resolve.

She looked at Cody.

"If you think his work will suit, hire him back. I'm sure not one to deny second chances. That's what I'm hoping for here–a second chance."

"Ranching's hard. It's no disgrace to choose another way to live," he said gently.

She smiled at him. "If it's so hard, why do you love it?"

He stared into her eyes.

"My mama always told us we could do hard things."

She laughed.

"I can't wait to meet your mother. She sounds very wise."

"They'll be gone a few more months. Apparently she's loving the cruise. I'm not so sure about my dad, but he'll do anything for her, so I guess he's satisfied."

"You're lucky to have both your parents still together and in love. My folks split when I was so little, I don't remember being a family. And neither ever remarried. Do you think that's odd?"

"Maybe they loved each other enough not to seek another mate, but just couldn't live together."

"Or maybe my mom just can't find a man rich enough to suit her," she said sarcastically. "She was always harping on seeking a rich man to marry. I think that's the wrong criteria. I want love, and friendship, and respect, and a real partnership."

She fell silent, gazing across the land. Cody was a partner. Cody fit the description of her ideal husband. She swallowed hard. She was afraid she was already in love with the cowboy.

And he probably still saw her as the spoiled daughter who had no idea she was bankrupting her father. Not someone he could respect, be friends with, fall in love with.

She sighed softly. Rising, she told him goodnight and hurried into the house. She'd do her best in the days ahead to show everyone she meant what she said. She'd turn this ranch into a profitable enterprise and make it a showplace. Her dad wasn't losing his home because of her!

15

At breakfast the next morning, Cody told Holly he'd called Ed when he got home last night and the man could move back once he'd given notice at his current job.

She glanced at Steve.

"How much longer do we get to have you here?" she asked.

"At least until Ed shows up, maybe another week after that. Cody's got some ideas that will require all hands on deck."

Holly looked at Cody, but he shrugged and kept eating. A minute later he spoke to the group.

"Speaking of all hands on deck, I'd like to get the rest of that spoiled hay out of the barn and get ready for a delivery. I've ordered five tons from the feed story and they can deliver next week. Then we need a new place to stockpile hay while the price is low. The barn will only hold so much."

Steve nodded. "There are some bales that aren't spoiled, so we separate. Where do you want the moldy hay?"

"Martin's Nursery in Coleville will take it. He sells it for composting. I think we can fill up my truck and if there's more, we'll fill Holly's truck. I'd like to get it out of here today if we can. It's supposed to rain tomorrow."

"Can do," Steve said.

Holly looked at the men.

"I can help with that, right?"

"Sure. We need the stalls mucked out first, cleaned and sprayed. I ordered more wood chips so we can put fresh bedding down when it's delivered."

He grinned at her. "Wear gloves or you'll have blisters on blisters."

When the men left to get started on removing the moldy hay, Holly quickly cleaned the kitchen. She was ready to head for the barn herself when the phone rang.

The hospital was calling, her dad's doctor was releasing him to return to the nursing home. They planned to transport him by ambulance and wanted to know if she could meet them at the nursing home that afternoon.

She arranged a time and went to let Cody know.

Mucking out stalls was fast becoming Holly's least favorite activity in the world. The old wood chips smelled, they were clingy, and they were heavy when wet. She shoveled wheel barrow load after load, trudging to the dump pile well behind the barn. Spreading it out to dry as instructed, she turned and headed back to the barn.

She was almost finished–literally and physically. Her arms ached. Her back was giving her fits. She kept at it. There was no way she was going to fall down on her first real assignment in working on the ranch. Cody had said it was hard. And his mom had said he could do hard things. She smiled at that, and knew she, too, could do hard things.

Keeping an eye out on the time, she wanted to make sure she had time to change clothes at least before heading to the nursing home this afternoon. Her father was due back there around three and she wanted to be there when he arrived.

She'd visited only a couple of times at the hospital. Both times he'd been asleep. She knew rest was probably the best thing, but wished she could talk to him, bring him up to speed on where they were on the ranch.

Had he fully understood the agreement she and Cody were ready to sign? She had her father's power of attorney, but still wanted to make sure he was okay with everything.

Cody was an easy going person. When her father was back in fighting form, surely the two of them could get along especially when each had the same goal with the ranch.

Holly arrived at the nursing home shortly before three. When she walked in, the administrator greeted her and said they were expecting her dad any minute. She showed Holly to his room and asked if she needed anything. When Holly said no, she left her there to return to her office.

Standing near the window, Holly gazed out at the pretty garden. Flowers were in full bloom. There was a walkway wide enough to accommodate wheelchairs. She wondered if her dad got to go outside if a nurse took him.

After spending time on the ranch, on the endless acres of wide open range, she could feel the closeness of the room, the garden. How did her dad stand it? She knew he'd much rather be on the back of a horse riding out to see to the cattle than lying in bed and going to physical therapy.

Her phone rang. She smiled when she heard her mom's voice. Sometimes she drove Holly up the wall, but she loved her mom and wish she was closer.

"Hi, Mom," she said.

"You must be in town to answer the phone. I have left three messages."

"Sorry, I forgot to check for messages when I got here."

"When are you coming home?"

"When will you stop asking?" Holly asked. "I'm staying here. I think for good."

"What? Stop being foolish. You'll hate the place as much as I do once you've been there a few weeks."

"Is that how long it took you to grow to hate it?"

Adrienne was quiet for a moment. "No, it was a bit longer. Winters are awful. Summers not much better. And the smell of cattle never went away."

Holly smiled. She rather liked the smell of cattle and horses. She'd never minded when she'd visited as a kid.

"I'm at the nursing home. Dad's due back any minute so I may have to go without any warning."

"How is your father," Adrienne asked.

"Not doing well. Before this second stroke the doctor wasn't giving me a prognosis that called for one hundred percent recovery. Now after a second stoke, I have no idea. I don't want him to die."

"Of course you don't, honey. Nor do I. As soon as he's able, he'll be back on that ranch. You'll see. He is the most stubborn man I know."

"I hope so. Anyway, I've gone into partnership with a local cowboy. We're working to bring the ranch around again."

"What? Does Frank know? Are you sure this cowboy isn't just trying to take you for a ride and acquire a ranch along the way?"

"He's from a neighboring ranch, so I think he knows what he's doing. And there are a lot of brothers on the ranch, so

I'm thinking he's glad to have part ownership in a ranch on his own."

"And how long before he owns the entire thing?"

"Mom, he's not after that. And we had an attorney draw up the agreement which states Dad can regain controlling interest when he's ready."

"I do believe you've lost whatever good sense you once had," her mother said.

"Oops, they're here. I've got to go. Love you."

Holly clicked off, glad for an excuse to end the call before she said something she'd regret.

In no time the ambulance attendants and one of the home's nurses had Frank settled in his hospital bed, cranked up so he could easily see Holly.

He smiled a lopsided smile at her and held out a shaky hand.

Holly grabbed it with both hers and smiled at her dad. He looked even thinner than the last time she'd seen him.

"You gave me another scare," she told him, sitting on the edge of the bed still holding his hand. "Let two strokes be your limit."

He nodded and said something, but the sounds didn't make sense and he frowned in frustration.

"I know, you were agreeing with me. So don't try to talk. I'll bring you up to speed on the ranch."

For the next few minutes Holly updated him on what she and Cody–mostly Cody– had done. Frank nodded a time or two. Holly wound down when she saw his eyes flickering.

"You're tired. Rest up. I'll come again soon. I need to pull my weight at the ranch, but I'm not going to skip visiting you."

He smiled again and tried to say something, but she couldn't understand him.

"Love you, Dad," she said, leaning over to kiss him. "Sleep now and get better really fast!"

He nodded, his eyes already closing.

She waited until she knew he was asleep and then slipped out of the room. Spotting the nurse down the hall she went over to her. "He's asleep and I didn't know how to lower the bed."

"I'll take care of it," the nurse said with a smile."

Holly climbed into the old truck ready to head for home when her phone rang again. This time it was Cody.

"How's your dad?" he asked.

Holly gave him a brief update.

"It's getting on toward supper time and you're sure to be tired so I called Carlos and told him to expect a bunch of us for dinner. Steve and Charlie and I are heading for the Rocking F when we finish here. Join us there for supper."

"That sounds wonderful."

She was delighted not to have to cook. Her arms still ached from the morning's work and she felt drained after talking with her mother and then seeing her dad.

When Holly arrived at the Rocking F she parked near the main house. She didn't see Cody's truck, so wasn't sure what she should do. Wait for him or go to the bunkhouse?

Seth Johnson came out to the porch and waved at her.

Glad for the welcome, Holly left the truck and approached the porch.

"Hi Seth," she said, glad for a friendly face.

"Welcome. I hear you and the rest of the Bar-B-Bar gang

will be eating with us. Good, you and the others can bring us up to date. How's your father?"

He gestured to the chairs on the porch and they sat while Holly updated him about her father.

"Sorry to hear that he's not recovering as fast as he probably wants. But Frank's tough, he'll get back in fighting shape, don't you worry."

"I sure hope so."

"Can I get you something to drink?" he asked.

"No, I'm fine. I'll wait for dinner. Which I'm glad I didn't have to fix today. It feels good to just sit for a little while." Her arms ached a little and she wanted nothing more than to have a hot bath and early bedtime. She was grateful not to have to prepare the evening meal for her cowboys.

Holly was happy to see Cody's truck when it turned to park next to hers. Her heart sped up a little and she relaxed.

Charlie climbed out of the passenger side. Steve's truck turned in next to Cody's.

"The gang's all here, I see," Holly said, jumping up.

"Hi Charlie. Did you get settled?" she asked walking over to the men.

"Dumped my stuff in one of the bedrooms. Horse is in the corral, so yeah, I'm set," he said.

Cody made introductions to his grandfather and suggested they head for the bunkhouse.

"Dinner will be ready soon," Seth said.

Cody fell into step with Holly.

"How's your dad?" he asked.

She updated him.

"But you're still worried," he said.

She nodded, blinking to keep tears at bay.

"He looked so frail. He's really not that old, is he? But he looked it today."

Cody reached out to encircle her shoulders and bring her close to him.

"He'll make it. From what I know of your dad, he's not one to give up. And think, with the hope of you staying around, I bet he's highly motivated to give it his all to get better."

"With the certainty of my staying," she murmured, relishing the strength she drew from Cody.

Holly was glad to see the cowboys of the Rocking F and remembered all their names this time. They welcomed her and the men from the Bar-B-Bar like they were all old friends. Well, in the case of Steve, they probably were. Dinner was entertaining once Pedro started with a wild story, and the rest picking up the unspoken challenge.

She laughed most of the evening and knew it was good for her. By the time they were ready to leave, she felt in much better spirits.

Leaving the bunkhouse, Cody asked for her keys.

She fished them out of her pocket and held them out.

"Why?" she asked.

"Charlie, you drive the ranch truck back. Steve's going home and I want to talk to Holly, so I'll bring her back."

Charlie caught the tossed keys and touched the edge of his hat in a friendly salute.

Holly looked at Cody.

"What do we need to talk about?" she asked.

"Anything you want. I wanted to be with you. I missed you today."

She giggled. "I was in the barn all morning as you were."

"Yeah, but then you left, maybe that's when I missed you," he said, holding open the passenger door to his truck.

"I should have driven back. Now you'll have to turn around and drive home," she said.

"Naw, I'll doss down in that second bedroom you cleaned," he said.

"Cody, do you have a minute?" Jarred asked, following them out.

Cody closed the passenger door and walked over to his brother.

"What's up?"

Jarred turned and began walking away from the truck, Cody following. "Is there a problem?"

"I hope not. Don't go falling for the gal," Jarred said. "I saw the way you looked at her tonight. She's not for the likes of us. She likes cities and parties and jetting around the world. She'll never settle—not on the Bar-B-Bar or anywhere out here."

"You don't know that," Cody replied, his tone mild even though anger was beginning to build.

"And you don't know that she'll stay, either." Jarred stopped walking and looked at Cody. "Don't make the mistake I made. If I can't talk you out of the path you've taken, at least don't do anything rash. Wait for mom and dad to come back."

"Why? Do you think Dad will talk some sense into me?" Cody asked, the anger edging his voice.

Jarred sighed and shook his head. "Just don't make a mistake."

Cody began walking toward the truck. "I won't be making any mistakes."

When he reached his truck, he took a deep breath. No sense in upsetting Holly.

In only moments they were driving down the dark road on the way to the Bar-B-Bar.

"My mom called while I was in town," Holly said. "She's convinced I won't stay that I'll get tired of being here in a few weeks. I don't believe that. I'm getting more and more frustrated when I say I'm staying and no one seems to believe me. My mom doesn't. I know your brother Jarred doesn't believe me, and I don't think you do either."

"Actually, I believe you believe that," Cody said in his defense.

"Well that's a real vote of confidence," she said sarcastically.

"Well, honey, look at it this way. This is totally different from what you've been accustomed to your whole life. It's also not even a normal time. You're worried about your dad, the ranch needs immediate infusion of hard work and cash. There are definite possibilities to bring about a big change in a short time but it's all foreign for you."

Holly hardly heard what he said focused on the one word at the start.

"What did you call me?" she asked, trying to see him in the dark.

He glanced her way. "Honey?"

"Why would you do that?"

"Cause you're the sweetest thing I know," he said gruffly.

She sat back in the seat, her heart racing. A slow smile grew.

The silence grew. Finally Cody said,

"Are you okay?"

"Oh, yes, cowboy, I'm very okay," she said.

She wondered if Cody could one day care for her like maybe in a few years when she was still here and he finally believed she'd stay.

"You know," she started, "the only way I know to prove I'm not leaving is not to leave."

"I guess."

"So what would it take to convince people? Two years? Ten? Fifty? I need to know a time frame so I'll know what to expect. In my own mind, I'm convinced. Have you ever felt out of place and not sure of what you're doing some place? That's how I felt in Europe. It was fun to see different capitals and the old architecture and museums. But I knew I didn't belong there. Then you end up where everything seemed perfect–not in the sense of being perfect–more in the sense of lining up and feeling right?"

He thought a moment. "Sort of. When I was in college I thought I wanted to be a cop."

"Really?" she couldn't picture him as anything other than what he was.

"Yeah, but then the criminal classes I took while interesting weren't really capturing me. Yet I couldn't soak up enough of the ag classes. Finally I gave up the idea of being a cop and it felt right. So I get what you're saying. Being here feels right."

"Exactly."

Maybe he'd really get it.

The lights were on in the bunkhouse when they reached the Bar-B-Bar. The ranch truck parked near the barn.

Cody walked her up to the back door and waited until she turned on the lights.

"Tomorrow we'll go into town and sign the agreement," he said.

"Then we'll be partners forever."

He hesitated a moment then nodded.

"Partners forever. Then I think I'll take you up on the offer of staying in the bunkhouse. Save driving back and forth."

"You'll be half owner so it makes sense."

"Good night, Holly."

He hesitated for a split second, then drew her into his arms and kissed her.

Her heart was on wings, her blood pounded and her mind turned to mush. She loved this cowboy who was practically a stranger, but whom she felt she'd known since before time. He was kind, honest, thoughtful and fun. His strength was something she could rely on.

The next morning Holly and Cody headed into town to see Nathan and sign their agreement. When they left the attorney's office, they headed to the bank.

"We'll fund the partnership account," Cody said as they entered the old building. The marble floors and ornate tellers counter attested to a bygone era when buildings were built to please the eye and not merely to be functional.

Patrice Canfield was crossing the lobby when she saw them.

"Hi Cody. What are you doing here?"

"Have you met Holly Braddock?" he asked.

When Patrice shook her head, Cody made introductions. "We're here to transfer some funds into the joint account for the Bar-B-Bar. Who do we see about that?"

"I can help. Though technically not my primary function, I'm glad to help a friend. Come on back to my office."

In no time Patrice had pulled up the account on her computer.

"How did you want to fund this? The balance currently is $50." she asked.

"I want to transfer some from my own account."

"Sure." She glanced at Holly but didn't say anything.

"So a hundred grand," Cody said.

Holly looked at him in astonishment.

"You're putting in one hundred thousand dollars?" she asked in disbelief.

"We need working capital," he said.

She blinked. Somehow in all this had she missed something? How could Cody have that much money in his account to transfer over? If he had that much ready cash why was he helping pull a rundown ranch from the brink?

She met Patrice's gaze and looked away. She could just imagine what the banker was thinking.

"All done. You can withdraw any time you want. There's no waiting period since both accounts are here. Anything else I can help you with?" she asked, sliding the receipt toward Cody.

Her question was directed at Cody.

Holly wanted to protest, or demand an explanation, or something.

"That's all for now. Thanks again."

He picked up the receipt and handed it to Holly.

They were both silent when they left the bank. She didn't speak until they were in the truck.

"How can you do that?" she asked.

"Do what?" He started the engine. "Want to try the barbecue place in Coleville?"

"Put so much money in the account."

"We need working capital."

"But that much?"

"I don't want to have to come into town every so often to transfer funds. This'll carry us for a while."

"That's for half interest in the ranch?"

He glanced at her. "Hardly. Just some working capital for us to use. How much do you think your dad's ranch is worth?"

"I don't know."

"My guess is upward to twenty times that."

She blinked.

"So my half when the appraisal comes through will be around ten million."

"Dollars?" she whispered.

He grinned. "Unless your dad wants another kind of currency."

"And you can pay ten million dollars for half share of the ranch."

He nodded.

"All at once?"

He nodded.

She stared out the windshield as he drove out of Wildcat

Creek heading for Coleville. Her mother had said the Fallons were rich. But she had no idea a cowboy who still technically lived at home had that kind of money available.

"What if it doesn't work?" she almost whispered.

"If what doesn't work?"

She looked at him. "How do you know we can save the ranch?"

He shrugged. "Instinct."

"What if I don't stay, like Jarred said?"

He smiled. "That's not who you are. You're in for the long haul. And I plan to be right there with you all the way."

Holly smiled as she kept her gaze forward. She was stunned to realize how much money Cody must have. That would take some getting used to. No wonder Jarred questioned her motives.

The barbecue place was half full when they arrived shortly past the lunch rush. They sat at a table near the back. Once they ordered, Cody asked her to tell him something about her year in Europe.

"What do you want to know?" she asked.

"Whatever struck you the most."

She thought a minute and then began with her first memories of landing in London. She told him of the beauty of architecture, museums with fabulous paintings and sculptures. How she managed with the local accents. Then gave a brief highlight of each country and city she visited.

Occasionally he'd ask a question for clarity but mostly he just watched her as she talked.

When the waitress brought their plates, Holly smiled.

"Enough. I've talked myself hoarse." she said.

"Fair enough. I love hearing your take on things. I think your dad did a good thing to let you experience all that. Most people never get the chance. Two weeks is the average vacation time unless you're a rancher. Then you're lucky to get a few days off."

"Your parents are taking more than a few days," she said, then took a bite of the ribs. A moan of delight followed.

He smiled and nodded.

"Good, huh? And my parents have been married more than thirty-five years and this is their first real vacation just the two of them. We traveled when I was a kid–mostly to states around Wyoming to visit National Parks. I loved those trips, but I think my mom would have preferred a luxury hotel to cooking over a camp fire."

Holly couldn't imagine cooking over a camp fire. She was lucky to cook basic foods on a gas range. The thought of that made her feel a bit down. She wasn't sure she could be a rancher's wife. There was a lot more than just feeding horses and cooking meals.

Not that she was thinking about becoming a rancher's wife. She was looking forward to the day her dad could come home. Together they'd work with Cody to make the ranch flourish.

"Now what are you thinking?" he asked.

"About when my dad might come home."

"And what if he doesn't?" he asked softly.

She looked at him.

"He's getting better," she said.

He nodded. "But better isn't complete recovery. I'm just saying that he might always need care. He may not recover fully enough to live independently. I'm hoping he'll make a full recovery. If he loves his ranch like my dad loves ours, he's missing it fiercely. And with the added bonus of his daughter being here, I know he's doing his best to get back one hundred percent. I'm just asking what will you do if he can't make it?"

She took a deep breath.

"I don't know. Continue to run the ranch. Bring him out for visits I guess. Hire a caretaker so he can live at home. I don't have all the answers to that situation. I'm still counting on him returning to his previous life."

Cody nodded.

"I like your answer. Especially having a caretaker live in. We could easily reconfigure the main floor for a bedroom and adjacent handicap bath."

Holly felt a burst of warmth at his saying we. She reached out and caught Cody's hand in hers and squeezed it slightly.

"Thank you. That means a lot that you're in this with me."

His hand turned over and clasped hers. "We're partners, remember."

"All for one and one for all?"

"Yep."

Holly stared into his bright blue eyes feeling warmth spread through her. After a minute, she smiled, withdrew her hand and began to eat the last of her meal.

Her heart raced. She wanted to gaze into Cody's eyes forever. But there was work to do, a ranch to save, and a promise to keep.

16

Cody drove back to Wildcat Creek after they finished lunch.

"I want to stop at the feed store and order hay. Jarred was saying the prices are the lowest he's seen this year, so I want to buy it now. It'll go up as fall approaches."

"Sounds fine. I'm anxious to get home and start making plans," she said gazing out the window to keep from staring at Cody.

They were the only people in the large barn-like building that housed the Wildcat Creek Feed and Grain. Joe was behind the counter and looked up when he saw Cody and then Holly.

"Hey, Cody. I haven't seen you in a while," the older man said.

"I know. Jarred's running things for the most part at the ranch until Dad gets back."

"How are things going out there?"

"Good. I'm here to order some hay for the Bar-B-Bar. Have you met Holly Braddock? She's Frank's daughter."

"Howdy," Joe said with a nod.

He looked at Cody. "There could be a problem. I, um, can't give you any credit."

He glanced at Holly then looked back to Cody.

"There's still a bit of a balance on the last charge from the Bar-B-Bar. You know how it is." He looked uncomfortable.

"No problem. We'll settle up the balance and pay cash for a discount for twenty tons of hay to be delivered sometime this week."

Joe studied him for a long moment. "Done deal. I'll give you a ten percent discount for cash."

"Done," Cody echoed.

Holly's faced burned with embarrassment with Joe's hesitancy to do business with the Bar-B-Bar. Every time something like this surfaced, she was reminded of her total unawareness of how much her father had sacrificed for her. And every time, it strengthened her resolve to change things.

When they arrived at the ranch, Holly was surprised to find a horse trailer parked in the area near the barn, and four new horses in the corral.

"Where did they come from?" she asked as she climbed out of the truck and walked to the corral.

Kyle Fallon came out of the barn.

"Hey," he called to them.

"Thanks," Cody said.

He looked at the horses. "How did Jarred let you take Thunder?"

Kyle laughed. "Ah, well, he doesn't exactly know yet."

Cody laughed with his brother. "I expect I'll hear about it."

"We're here to help. Hey Holly."

"Kyle," she acknowledged his greeting. "What are these horses doing here?"

"Cody said you needed some new stock until the ranch

can buy some. We don't really need these horses until later in the fall, so might as well keep them working here so they don't get fat and lazy."

"And Thunder?" she asked, curious.

"Well, he's the best cutting horse we've got. We don't need his expertise right now. That'll come in the fall roundup. So now he can get some practice in here when you start culling the herd," Kyle explained.

"Culling the herd?" she asked, looking at Cody.

"One of the things to discuss." He looked at Kyle. "I appreciate the loan. As soon as we get some horses, we'll bring them back."

"As long as they are back when fall comes, it's all good."

"I don't envy you when Jarred finds out."

Kyle laughed again. "Yeah, well, you could come to dinner again and watch."

"No, thanks. We're going to begin building camaraderie and loyalty for the Bar-B-Bar. We've hired one new cowhand and Ed's coming back. Walt loaned us a cowboy. So we've got enough for a start. Still looking for another to replace Steve when he goes back to Walt's. Anyone you know looking?"

Kyle shook his head. "I'll check around. Someone might turn up."

"We've got enough for a start, four and a half."

"A half?" Kyle asked.

"Holly's a half. She also does the cooking and so can't work all day on the range."

Cody looked at her and smiled. She smiled back.

While not thrilled with the idea of cooking for everyone every day, it beat ten or twelve hours in the saddle. She was grateful to be a half.

"It's good to see you, Kyle. But speaking of cooking means I need to get inside and see what I can come up with for dinner. Want to stay?"

"No, thanks. Another time, maybe. I need to get back. Plan on coming to the ranch next week. Bring your crew if you like."

Kyle bid them goodbye and got in the big truck. Backing around, soon the truck and large horse trailer pulled out of the yard.

"After dinner, I want to hear more about culling the herd," she said to Cody, and then turned to walk to the house.

Thankful that the Bar-B-Bar didn't have as many ranch hands as the Rocking F, Holly began planning meals for the next week or so. There were still some items in the big chest freezer, but she wanted to make a list of groceries and after visiting her father tomorrow, she'd swing by the store and purchase enough food to last a week or more.

Dinner was a hit with each man eating at least twice what she did. She was glad there was plenty. Meat, potatoes, vegetables and lots of biscuits. The men weren't fussy and she knew they liked this kind of food compared to the lighter meals she usually enjoyed.

Another change for ranch life.

After the dishes were washed and put away, Holly and Cody went into the office to discuss plans for the ranch. Cody outlined the ideas he had and the priority he wanted for each one. They discussed each suggestion. Holly agreed. He knew so much more about what was needed and in what order. She was glad to agree.

For each idea, she silently added the estimated costs. The

one hundred thousand dollars in the joint account wouldn't last forever. She made sure Cody knew her top priority was the salaries of the men.

"I don't want Ed to bad mouth us all over again," she said.

"Me, either. Before long this ranch and all its owners will have a stellar reputation. Your dad is respected in the community. Everyone can relate to things changing because of ill health."

She smiled at him. "Thank you for coming over that first day. Who knows where I'd be now if you hadn't. Your grandfather told me you were reluctant and wanted one of the others to come. But I'm so glad it was you."

He looked away. In retrospect, he was glad his grandfather had insisted.

"I'll go in with you tomorrow to see your dad. We'll run everything by him. He can't talk too well right now, but I bet his mind is as sharp as ever. He is entitled to veto anything he doesn't like."

She nodded, unexpectedly touched by Cody's sense of right. Another man would have taken over and waited for her dad to totally recover.

It was late when they were finished.

"Is this everything?" she asked, her head swimming with numbers and to do lists, and the enormity of the tasks ahead.

"For now," he said, standing. "We'll get these behind us and then discuss other jobs like repainting the house, bunkhouse and barn. Keeping up appearances and protecting the wood from the weather will have to wait a bit, but it'll happen."

She looked up at him, excited about the possibility of

fixing up the structures. The corral had already been repaired. She couldn't wait until they started on the house. But that wasn't even on their current priority list. Patience might be hard to come by.

"Walk me out?" he asked.

"Sure. It's late. What time should I expect you tomorrow?"

"I've been bringing clothes and things each day, so now I'm officially moved into the bunkhouse. So I'll be in for breakfast with the rest of the crew."

"So another reason for Jarred not to favor me," she said softly.

He laughed. "Don't worry about Jarred. If they need me at the Rocking F they can call. We'll help each other out at roundups, and maybe when the Rocking F cuts hay. But for the near future, that ranch will function fine without me."

They stepped out into the night. There were lights on in the bunkhouse. The rest of the ranch lay in darkness with only the brilliance of the star-studded sky to offer faint illumination.

Cody cupped her face in his hands and kissed her. "Sleep well," he said, stepping away and heading toward the bunkhouse.

Holly watched him until he stepped inside the bunkhouse. Her heart raced. It would be hard to go right to sleep. Daydreams and fantasies bubbled up in her mind. Trying to be practical, she turned and went inside. Morning came early.

The next morning Holly wanted to turn over and go back to sleep when her alarm went off. But days of sitting around and doing nothing were now a memory. She had to get breakfast for a some hungry men.

Dressed and in the midst of preparing a large breakfast, she was glad she didn't have to feed the horses at this early hour. With more men on the ranch, chores were being delegated and she was pleased to be relieved of that particular one. Especially if it was as cold as her mother said in winter.

And she was taking pride in preparing hearty meals. The compliments were welcomed. She hid her uncertainty and with every meal felt more proficient. She especially liked the way Cody's face lit up when he saw her each morning.

Once everyone had been served, Cody took a few bites and then looked at the others.

"Holly and I are going into town as soon as we can to see her father. We've made a list of what we want accomplished and in what order, so once Frank signs off, we'll all discuss things. We'll have one more hand starting and I've asked him to join us at dinner to hear the plans. If you have something you feel you're especially proficient at, let me know so I can tailor tasks to best suit everyone."

"I won't be staying once Ed starts," Steve said.

"I know. We'll still need another man to replace you."

"Thank you for all you've done," Holly said. "Tell Walt I owe him. And I owe you,"

He nodded, then grinned. "You can bake me some brownies now and then. And I know Walt favors brownies as well."

"Done. Might be my contribution to the efforts–brownies once a week."

The men told her they'd love that.

As soon as the men left, with their bag lunches, Holly hurried to clean up. Cody had gone with the rest, but she knew he'd be back when time to go to see her father.

When it was time, Cody said he'd take his truck while she drove hers.

"I have some errands to run and don't want to go grocery shopping. Soon as I'm finished, I can head back here. That way you can take your time shopping and get all you need."

"Okay."

Holly was disappointed they wouldn't be riding together. She had looked forward to more time with him, just the two of them.

Frank had finished breakfast when they entered his room. His lopsided smile rose when he saw Holly and then Cody.

They quickly reviewed all the plans made the previous evening. From time to time Frank nodded. He tried to speak but the frustration when the words wouldn't come riled him up. Cody told him if he objected to anything just raise his hand. Frank shook his head and raised a fist with the thumb up.

In a short time after getting agreement on the plans, Holly rose.

"You're getting tired, Dad, and I have a lot of shopping to do. You can't imagine how much these cowboys eat. I'm hoping to get enough to last at least a week."

She leaned over and gave him a kiss on the forehead. "Keep getting well."

She looked at Cody.

"I'll be leaving in a couple of minutes. I want to talk to your dad about something."

"Okay, see you back at the ranch."

"When you get back to the ranch, if I'm not around, come find me. I'll be on the east side on that stretch of fence that borders the Rocking F."

She nodded and walked out. Secretly pleased he had confidence in her finding him, she hoped she could do it. If in doubt, she could figure out east and just ride until she found the fence then follow it.

It was almost time for lunch by the time Holly returned with her pick up truck loaded with everything she needed for a week and a half of meals. It took time to put everything away, but she was pleased at how full the shelves and freezer were once she was done.

After a hasty lunch, she grabbed her hat and walked out to the barn. Several horses dozed in the corral. She took a halter and called Starlight. Proud she could get the horse saddled up, she led her to a block Cody had put near the barn so she could easily mount.

Settling in the saddle she studied the sky and headed out.

Elation filled her when some time later she saw Cody and Steve working on a section of fence.

"This must be the eastern fence," she murmured, urging her horse to a faster pace.

When she reached the men, her face was flushed and she was grinning. She'd done it!

Cody grinned at her. "Good job. Can you dismount by yourself?" he teased.

"You bet."

She slid off the horse holding on to the saddle horn for a moment to make sure her legs would hold her.

"What are you doing here? Was the fence broken?" She looked at the difference in one section.

"Naw, we've fixed the gate. Rocking F has a portion of Wildcat Creek running through. I told you it's good swimming on these hot days. Now you and me and rest of the Bar-B-Bar crew can take advantage of some cooling off when work's done."

"Better than a swimming pool," Steve added. "I'm going over to check it out."

The gate looked to Holly like poles and barbed wire, but she saw how it was opened and then closed to keep cattle in.

Once Steve rode out of sight, Cody fastened the wire around the two poles that butted up to each other and gathered the tools they'd used, wrapping them in a leather carry-all.

"Nice. When do we get to go swimming? It's hot enough today," she asked.

"We have to set things up with the Rocking F. In the past unless my Mom was coming, it was a free for all for guys only. When we plan to go we need to give some warning."

She laughed. "So no skinny dipping when I'm there."

"Right."

She turned and looked around. The air was hot, the sun blazing, the smell of drying grass and faintly of cattle filled her lungs. Who knew she'd grow to love that so quickly. She and her mother were so different. She now couldn't imagine living anywhere else.

"What are you thinking?" Cody asked, tying the carry all to the back of his horse.

"How different my mom and I are. She loves the city,

shopping, visiting friends. But I'm loving this. I wonder if that is because I'm half my dad and the heritage of this land is in my bones."

Cody stepped next to her.

"Holly," he said, then stopped.

She turned and smiled up at him. "What?"

"Would you marry me? Marry me and live here forever?"

She blinked, totally stunned at his words.

He rushed into speech when she didn't respond.

"I know we haven't know each other for long and we can be engaged as long as you like. We for sure can't get married until my folks get home and your dad's better. But I knew almost the first moment I saw you that you were someone I wanted to get to know. Someone I've fallen in love with. I've never felt this way about anyone before. I promise."

"Oh, Cody," she said softly.

"Don't say no. Think about it for a while."

"I don't need to think about it. I love you, too. I'd be honored to be your wife."

She scarcely had the words out of her mouth before he drew her into his arms and kissed her like never before.

The sun was blazing but the heat Cody brought was fiercer. Endless moments suspended in time while she relished the feel of this cowboy. Agreeing to marry him seemed the best thing that she'd ever done.

He broke the kiss and rubbed a thumb across her flushed cheek.

Fumbling in a pocket, he brought out a sparkling diamond ring.

"I guessed at the size," he said, reaching for her hand and slipping the ring on her finger. It fit perfectly.

"It's beautiful," she said, tears in her eyes.

"If you don't like it, we can exchange it for something else. I made sure of that before I bought it."

"I love it. It's the most beautiful ring ever. I'll be so happy to wear it the rest of my life."

Cody let out a sigh.

She peeked up at him. "Don't tell me you were nervous."

"Heck yeah, I had no idea if you'd be at all interested."

"I don't kiss other men like you and I have kissed. That could have been a clue."

She tilted her hand in the sun, seeing the rainbow in the stone. "I bet my dad's going to be surprised."

Cody cleared his throat.

"He may be at your answer, but I asked his permission to ask you."

She looked at him. "You did? That's so incredibly sweet."

"He said I could and I expect if he could have spoken clearly would have warned me to make sure you were happy all your days."

She laughed. "And I will be with you."

She stepped closer and hugged him.

"And I do need to go tell Dad. We can go after dinner. And take some sparkling cider. He could drink that I'm sure. Oh, and I need to call my mother."

For a moment Holly hesitated. Her mom would not be happy. But maybe in a few years seeing how happy her daughter was with Cody, she'd come around.

But if not, so be it. It wouldn't change her love for this wonderful man.

"We can fly to California to tell her if you like," he offered.

"No, but thanks for the suggestion. There's too much to do here."

"Spoken like a true rancher."

He kissed her again.

"Have you told your family?" she asked.

"Not yet. I wanted to make sure of your answer first. We'll have to tell them the next time my folks call in. I'm sure grandpa will be delighted. He's the one who encouraged me to check out the ranch in the first place."

She smiled. She remembered how reluctant he seemed when they first met. How things had changed.

"Was this why you suggested the partnership with the ranch?" she asked.

"I thought it would be a good way to get to know you better, have you know what life here is like. But I knew almost that first day that you were the one for me."

"I feel like I'm floating I'm so happy."

"I want you to be happy the rest of your life," he said softly and kissed her again.

Their special moment ended when Cody finally pulled back. "Things to do."

"Right. Can we tell the men at dinner?"

"It's not a secret. We can drive over to the Rocking F and let them know after dinner. Knowing Wildcat Creek, it'll be all over town before we can blink twice."

She laughed. "Fine by me."

She reached up for a quick kiss and then turned to her horse. "Can you please help me up? I ought to float up into the saddle, but I think gravity won't let me."

Ed came to dinner that night. He spoke to Holly privately to apologize for his comments around town when he'd left without being paid for a few weeks. She apologized that it happened and promised he could count on his pay being made up and for future checks paid without fail in the future. The flashing diamond caught Charlie's eye and congratulations were quickly offered by all the cowboys. Cody received several slaps on the back for his congratulations.

Once dinner was finished, everyone went to the living room where Cody outlined the plans for the near future. There was discussion, chores divvied up, ideas explored, and new lists drawn up.

After the men left, Cody and Holly piled into his truck and headed for the Rocking F.

"Jarred's not going to be happy," she said as they turned onto the long drive to the ranch house.

"You're not marrying Jarred," he commented. "Sometimes I think he's never going to get over his broken engagement. He's grown so cynical since then. It gets old."

When they entered the house, they heard voices in the dining room. Everyone was gathered around a laptop and talking to someone there.

"Serendipity," Cody murmured stepping in and leaning over to be seen by the camera. "Hey," he said.

Kyle moved to one side so Cody could move closer. His hand held Holly's and he pulled her close.

"Got some news," he said. "This is Holly Braddock, Frank's daughter."

"Hello, Holly," Marge Fallon said on the computer. "How's your father doing? We were so shocked to hear about his stroke."

"Hi. He's doing better. It'll be a long recovery but we're hoping a full one."

She smiled shyly at the camera.

"I've got an announcement," Cody said, leaning a bit closer to the computer.

"Holly's agreed to marry me."

The exclamations overlapped. Someone said What? Another I don't believe it. His mom looked stunned for a moment, then smiled broadly.

"Wonderful news. When did this happen?" she asked.

His father's face filled the screen. "Hi, Holly, welcome to the family."

"Today, I asked her today and she said yes," Cody said.

"You didn't set a wedding date yet did you?" His mother's face reappeared. "I need to be there."

"We didn't," Holly said. "We have to wait for you two to get back home and for my dad to get well enough to walk me down the aisle. A wedding needs all the family there."

"Oh I have to many questions. And our time is almost up," Marge said. "It'll be a few days before our next port of call. I hope I can wait. So nice to meet you Holly," she said.

Two minutes later the computer screen went black.

Seth turned to Holly.

"I echo my son-in-law's greeting, welcome to the family." He gave her a warm hug.

Jarred made a scoffing sound and quickly left the room. A moment later the front door slammed.

Holly looked at Cody who was talking with Kyle. He caught her eye and winked.

Her mother and Jarred. Would either come around? Time would tell.

The drive back to the Bar-B-Bar was quiet. It was late. Holly touched her ring and smiled, happiness still filling every inch. She tried to see Cody in the illumination from the dash. Soon to be her husband, partner, best friend. They would build a wonderful life on the ranch. Build a family.

"Do you want kids?" she asked.

"I do, A bunch. How about you?" he replied easily.

"Yes. A new generation to bond with the land and carry on the traditions of our families into the future."

"Agreed." He reached out and took her hand, lacing his fingers through hers. "I love you, Holly."

"I love you, Cody."

Even though darkness surrounded them in the night, the future looked as bright as the noonday sun.

—The End—

If you liked **Holly's Reluctant Cowboy**,
you'll love **Patrice's Remarkable Cowboy**,
book 4 in the Cowboys of Wildcat Creek series.

If you enjoyed **Holly's Reluctant Cowboy**,
please consider leaving a review.

More books by Barbara McMahon

Cowboys of Wildcat Creek
Valentine's Cowboy Rescue
Shelly and the Cowboy
Kristi's Cowboy Hero
Holly's Reluctant Cowboy
A Cowboy for Eliza

Sweet Reunion Romance Collection
Unexpected Reunion
Unpredictable Reunion
Unanticipated Reunion

The Talmadge Sisters
Letters to Caroline
Michelle's Marriage Deal
Trusting Abby

The Harts of Texas Series
Rebel Heart
Tangled Hearts
Reckless Heart

Cowboy Heroes Series
Blue Bells on the Hill
Cowboy's Bride
One Stubborn Cowboy
Crazy About a Cowboy
Never Doubt a Cowboy
Cowboy Marshal
Summer Cowboy
Second Chance Cowboy
Movie Star Cowboy

Tropical Escape Series
Island Rendezvous
Come into the Sun
Island Paradise

Tropical Escape Series
Island Rendezvous
Come into the Sun
Island Paradise

Rocky Point Series
Rocky Point Legacy
Rocky Point Reunion
Rocky Point Promise
Rocky Point Hero
Rocky Point Inn
Rocky Point Dawn

The Ultimate Billionaires
The Cynical Sheikh
Falling for the Sheikh
A Sheikh of Her Own
The Unforgettable Sheikh

Sweet Romance Stand-alone Collection
Because of You
Cowboy Charade
I'll Take Forever
Jared's Promise
Mail Order Bride
Not Really Married
Sweet Meant To Be
The Cowboy Comes Home
The Paper Marriage
Trusting Jake
The Banished Bride

A Sweet Clean Christmas Romance Collection
The Christmas Cop
The Cowboy's Special Christmas
A Soldier's Christmas
A Teaspoon of Mistletoe
The Christmas Locket
A Key West Christmas